R.L. 5.8

#116,359

P9-DET-293

DATE DUE

APR 1 2 2018	

DEMCO, INC. 38-2931

Miss *Spitfire*

REACHING HELEN KELLER

Sarah Miller

ATHENEUM BOOKS FOR YOUNG READERS

NEW YORK   LONDON   TORONTO   SYDNEY

If you purchased this book without a cover, you should be aware that
this book is stolen property. It was reported as "unsold and destroyed"
to the publisher, and neither the author nor the publisher has
received any payment for this "stripped book."

ATHENEUM BOOKS FOR YOUNG READERS
An imprint of Simon & Schuster Children's Publishing Division
1230 Avenue of the Americas, New York, New York 10020
This book is a work of fiction. Any references to historical events,
real people, or real locales are used fictitiously. Other names,
characters, places, and incidents are products of the author's imagination,
and any resemblance to actual events or locales or persons,
living or dead, is entirely coincidental.
Copyright © 2007 by Sarah Miller
All rights reserved, including the right of reproduction
in whole or in part in any form.
ATHENEUM BOOKS FOR YOUNG READERS is a registered trademark
of Simon & Schuster, Inc.
For information about special discounts for bulk purchases,
please contact Simon & Schuster Special Sales at 1-866-506-1949
or business@simonandschuster.com.
The Simon & Schuster Speakers Bureau can bring authors to your live event.
For more information or to book an event, contact the
Simon & Schuster Speakers Bureau at 1-866-248-3049
or visit our website at www.simonspeakers.com.
Also available in an Atheneum Books for Young Readers hardcover edition.
Book design by Krista Vossen
The text for this book is set in Bodoni Twelve.
Manufactured in the United States of America
0916 OFF
First Atheneum Books for Young Readers paperback edition August 2010
10 9 8
The Library of Congress has cataloged the hardcover edition as follows:
Miller, Sarah Elizabeth, 1979–
Miss Spitfire / Sarah Miller
p. cm
Summary: At age twenty, partially-blind, lonely but spirited Annie Sullivan
travels from Massachusetts to Alabama to try and teach six-year-old Helen
Keller, deaf and blind since age two, self-discipline and communication skills.
Includes historical notes and timeline. Includes bibliographical references.
ISBN 978-1-4169-2542-2 (hc)
1. Sullivan, Annie, 1866–1936–Juvenile fiction. 2. Keller, Helen, 1880–1968–
Juvenile fiction. [1. Keller, Helen, 1880–1968–Fiction. 2. Sullivan, Annie, 1866–
1936–Fiction. 3. Blind–Fiction. 4. Deaf–Fiction. 5. People with disabilities–
Fiction. 6. Teachers–Fiction. 7. Alabama–History–1819–1950–Fiction.] I. Title.
PZ7.M63443Mis 2007
[Fic]–dc22
2006014738
ISBN 978-1-4424-0851-7 (pbk)
ISBN 978-1-4424-0724-4 (eBook)

For my grandpa, Harold Gass, who honors his teachers and knows about devotion

> *I feel sure that, if you write this book, I shall know you deeply for the first time. . . . I have always realized that there are chapters in the book of your personality which remain sealed to me.*
>
> —HELEN KELLER TO ANNE SULLIVAN, 1916

Deep in the grave our dust will stir at what is written in our biographies.

—Anne Sullivan, August 23, 1934

Miss Spitfire

Chapter 1

The man who sold us that ticket ought to be hanged,
and I'd be willing to act as hangman.

—ANNE SULLIVAN TO SOPHIA HOPKINS, MARCH 1887

"Ticket, please."

I wipe at my eyes and thrust the wretched thing at him. I've already had to change trains six times since Boston. On top of that, I have to take this train north to Knoxville to catch yet another train south to Alabama.

The conductor examines the ticket and punches it. Instead of returning it, he lingers over my shoulder. With a sniff I try to smother my tears before my handkerchief soaks up all my dignity.

"You all right, miss?" he asks.

I glance up at him and nod. He doesn't budge. He only stares. I can see him thinking it. Everyone who meets me thinks it, whether they say it or not.

She'd be pretty if it weren't for those eyes.

Sometimes I wonder if it was worth all those

operations. What good is being able to see if everyone who looks at me has to force the disgust from their lips at the sight of my poor eyes? And what a sorry sight they are—red and swollen, as if I were a demon straight from the underworld. There wasn't much good in being half blind and cross-eyed, either; but at least I couldn't see people staring at me.

"Is something wrong?" I snap at him. I can't help myself—my eyes smart with coal dust, I'm sweating in my woolen dress, and my patience is worn raw as my feet after tramping through Washington, DC, in too-tight new shoes.

He blinks in surprise. "No, ma'am. It's just you've been crying since we pulled outta Chattanooga. I thought maybe one of your folks was dead."

I don't know how to answer him. Most all of them are dead, and the living ones might as well be, for all they care about me. Even the dead ones aren't worth a tear.

Except for Jimmie.

"No, I'm going to Alabama. To teach."

He brightens. "Well, isn't that nice! I've got a cousin lives down that way. You'll like it there." He reaches into his pocket. "Peppermint?"

"I've never been outside of Massachusetts," I whimper, cringing all the while at the attention I've drawn.

"Oh, I shouldn't worry about that. Southerners are good people, real kind. Famous for our hospitality." He winks and holds the handful of candy still and steady, like I'm a sparrow he's trying to tame. I pick a small one and drop it into my pocket.

"Thank you."

"Go on, have another."

His voice makes the words soft and lazy—I like the way he says "anutha." Against my better judgment I concede a smile and take a larger piece.

"There, now. That wasn't so bad, was it?"

I shake my head.

"I see plenty of people come down here from up north. Stiff and prim as whitewashed fence pickets, every one of 'em. We smooth 'em out, though. Sunshine and country cooking turns 'em all bright and rosy in no time. Why, my mother used to put brown sugar in near about everything she made." He pats his sides. The cloth round his waistcoat buttons puckers. "Didn't do me any good around the middle, but we all grew up sweet and gentle as milch cows."

As he speaks, I mop my sooty eyes, only half listening. He takes it for more tears, I suppose.

"You'll make a fine teacher," he insists in that frantic way men get when a woman cries.

"I don't *want* to teach," I hiccup. That stops him cold for a second, then he's off again, prattling on about his sister-in-law who's a teacher, how it'll grow on me, and how I should give it a chance. Then he winks and says the most ridiculous thing of all: "Some of the boys might be sweet on you."

I have half a mind to tell him I have no training

and I'd rather be selling books door-to-door, or even washing dishes at Mrs. D's Kitchen in Boston, thank you very much. I won't have a classroom, either, only one pupil—a six-year-old girl both deaf and blind. What would he say to that, I wonder? But he's trying to be kind to me, and I know that's no easy task. I swallow my temper and unwrap one of the peppermints. Its cool sting helps ease the thickness in my throat.

"Thank you," I tell him. What I mean is *Go away*.

"That's better, isn't it?" he says, as if he's talking to a child. "Would you like a sandwich?"

I look him square in the eye, making the words firm and distinct: "No. Thank you."

He hovers a moment longer, then finally seems to sense I'd like it very much if he left me alone. "All right, then. You enjoy the ride, now."

Enjoy the ride. I wish he hadn't said that. So far I've managed not to remember the last time I rode a train.

Suddenly I'm nine years old again.

◦　◦　◦

My mother is dead and my drunken lout of a father is too busy giving the Irish a bad name to be bothered with his own children. Aunt Ellen snatches up cuddly, healthy baby Mary, but my brother and I are a problem. Jimmie's sickly and crippled; I'm mostly blind and surly as a wildcat. Finally we're dropped into the reluctant hands of Uncle John and his wife, Anastasia.

After a few months of my rages and Jimmie's frailty, their Christian charity runs out.

One day a carriage appears in the yard.

Uncle John lifts Jimmie onto the seat, his voice dripping with false cheer. He tells us we're going to have a ride on a train, and won't that be grand?

He doesn't tell us where the train is going. Or why no one else is coming.

I turn suspicious when Aunt Stasia tries to kiss me. She's never shown us any affection before, and I won't have it now. I twist my head away, and she dries her tears on her apron as if I've finally given her reason to hate me. "You might at least be a good girl on the last day," she sniffs as Uncle John hoists me into the seat next to Jimmie. My skin prickles for an instant at that, "the last day," but Uncle John makes such a fuss about shining locomotives and soft velvet seats that I forget to be afraid.

As the carriage rattles away down the road, one of the cousins calls out, "Enjoy the ride!"

Chapter 2

*But I was too anxious to take very much
interest in what I saw.*

—ANNE SULLIVAN TO SOPHIA HOPKINS, MARCH 1887

The memories make me so restless I'm almost glad to switch trains in Knoxville. I may know where this train is taking me, but I don't feel any more prepared for this journey than I was for the one that took me from Uncle John's to Tewksbury.

How do I dare hope to teach this child–Helen–when I've never taught a child who can see and hear? I've only just graduated from Perkins Institution for the Blind myself. Worse, it's not simply that Helen can't hear words or see signs–she lost her sight and hearing as a baby, before she learned language. The very notion that words exist, that objects have names, has never occurred to her. It's up to me to show her that communication between people exists at all. My mind wobbles at the thought of it. At least I know the task isn't impossible; Perkins's famous Dr. Howe taught my own cottage mate Laura Bridgman to communicate half a century ago, and she's both deaf and blind.

Even so, I'm afraid. After years of being blind myself, I can understand a mind without pictures, but I can hardly comprehend a mind without words. Words, songs, stories—they were the things I craved most before my sight was restored, for words explained the things my eyes couldn't show me. When I was blind, words were as vital as breath.

Closing my eyes, I try to form a wordless thought with the few tools Helen can use: shape, size, texture, scent, and taste. Without much trouble I conjure up a mind-feeling for an apple: round, firm, and smooth, with a soapy-sweet scent that fills my mouth.

But I have to fight to keep the words from my thoughts. My mind aches to say "apple." As that wordless apple-feeling hovers in my head, it's like holding my breath to keep my brain from reminding me, *No words, no words, only sensations.* No matter how I try, I can't silence that voice in my head. Even when I block "apple" from my mind, streams of thoughts whir in the background, as if my brain can't bear not whispering to itself. When I finally give up, a cold worry has twisted its way into my stomach.

How am I to teach Helen what language is, when words themselves have no scent, taste, or texture?

Seeking comfort, I run my fingers over the ring Mr. Anagnos, the director of Perkins, gave me before I left. Its stone is a deep, smoky red, like subdued flames—a fine choice for the unruly girl they used to call Miss Spitfire. The stone shines back at me like a beacon.

No matter how many doubts I confess, Mr. Anagnos has shown me nothing but enthusiasm for this position. Perhaps he's simply happy to be washing his hands of me at last. My housemother—Mrs. Hopkins—and my teachers have all been kind and encouraging, though I wouldn't be surprised to find them laughing in their sleeves at the idea of Annie Sullivan undertaking any child's education. Only Laura Bridgman herself has high hopes for me. The thought of it all makes my fingers twitch and my heart race as the train lumbers toward Tuscumbia.

I throw an anxious stare out the window. The grass grows greener and the leaves larger as we trudge south. I manage a wavery smile, remembering the snow I left behind in Boston. Redbuds and forsythias bloom along our path, but they're no more than a blur to me. My mind is tangled with uncertainties.

Despite all my grumbling, I'm anxious to meet my little pupil, if only to quell my fears. Until I see her for myself, there's nothing for me to do but wonder and worry. What if Helen's like Laura Bridgman, whose eerie manner leaves everyone in our cottage unnerved and exhausted? Laura reminds me more of a clockwork toy than a person—either flitting about in an agitated way, as if her key has been turned too far, or sitting still and solemn as a pocket watch with its mainspring unwound. If Helen is at all like Dr. Howe's pupil, my nerves will desert me entirely before the week is out.

More than that, I'm afraid Helen's family expects too much from me. If they've read the newspaper articles about Laura, they're prepared for a miracle. They don't know Laura's "miraculous" education was hardly perfect. It's true she learned to communicate, but her sentences are strange, as though her thoughts have been translated from an unknown language or strung together by a machine. Even if I manage to duplicate Dr. Howe's success, there's no guarantee the Kellers will be satisfied.

Which reminds me of the most worrisome problem of all: No one, not even Dr. Howe himself, has repeated his achievement in the fifty years since he and Laura made history. I've read all of his reports on Laura, and I know his methods like the Our Father, but except for Laura, Dr. Howe's methods failed with every deaf-blind student he met. If the Kellers are hoping for another Laura Bridgman, I don't know how I—an untrained Irish orphan—can please them. I can't tell them there may never be another Laura Bridgman; I can't afford to lose this job.

I have nowhere else to go.

There's not a relative alive who'd have me, and I wouldn't know where to find them now anyhow. I'd die of shame if I had to go back to Perkins a failure. Just to get on this train I had to borrow the fare from Mr. Anagnos. Besides, the way some of the institution's benefactors see it, I overstepped my welcome among the blind students and teachers the moment my sight was restored. Even then there was nowhere to send me but back into the hands of the state, and incorrigible as I was, not one of them had the heart to do that.

Like a forlorn child, I wish for the doll that's packed away in my trunk. The blind girls at Perkins pooled their pocket money to buy it for Helen, and Laura Bridgman herself sewed the clothes for it with her cool, thin hands. I'm eager to give it to Helen, yet at the same time part of me wants it for myself. I've never had a doll of my own, and my lonely heart tells me this trip might be easier if I had something to hold on to. At least at Tewksbury I had Jimmie, for a little while.

Tewksbury.

For most people it's only a name. They know, in a formal way, it's the Massachusetts state almshouse. They think it's a shame people end up there. They read about it in the newspaper, sigh and shake their head, then turn the page.

It's not like that for me. Tewksbury was nearly five years of my life. I almost thank God I was too blind to see most of it.

* * *

When Jimmie and I arrive, they try to separate us. "Boy to the men's ward, girl to the women's," they bark.

Jimmie whimpers. I fight. Like a beast, I kick and scratch and tear at them. I scream like the banshees in the stories my father told when he was only drunk enough to be cheerful.

They relent and send us both to the women's ward,

though Jimmie has to suffer wearing a girl's apron. We spend the first night in the dead house, unaware of the corpses piled about us.

Little changes about our lives when we're sent to Tewksbury. We're used to being poor and unwanted. We've always known drab and shabby rooms. All we have to adjust to is the constant hum of the insane, the laughter of whores, and the clatter of the metal cart that hauls the bodies to the dead house.

Our days form a pattern. We play in the dead house, cutting out paper dolls and taunting the rats with our scraps of paper. We learn to avoid the touch of the deranged and diseased. We play with the foundlings before they wither and die.

It's not such a bad life.

We have each other.

Until May.

The lump on Jimmie's hip grows until he can't stand up without screaming from the pain. A doctor is summoned. He bends over Jimmie's bed, then puts his hand on my shoulder and says, "Little girl, your brother will be going on a long journey soon." When I sense his meaning, more from his voice than his words, terror sweeps over me and cruel fingers grip my heart. The pain makes me beat out at the doctor in a rage. Scowling at me like I'm a grotty dishrag he can't be bothered with, the doctor seizes my arms and threatens to send me from the ward. I cease my clawing and surrender instantly. I'll let no one but God separate us.

And He does.

I'm sound asleep when they roll Jimmie's bed into the dead house. When I wake and sense the emptiness in the dark where his bed should be, I'm filled with wild fear—I know Jimmie is dead, as surely as I know where they've taken him. But my anger is gone, and with it my strength. Only crippling dread remains. I can't get out of bed, my body shakes so violently.

Somehow I calm myself and make my way to the door of the dead house. The sound of its latch starts the trembling all over again. I feel my way to Jimmie's bed and pull myself up on the iron rail. I touch his cold little body under the sheet, and something in me breaks.

My screams wake the whole ward.

*　　*　　*

The very thought of it makes me tremble. I clutch at my bag and struggle to do as Tim, the driver who took me from the almshouse to Perkins, told me: "Don't ever come back to this place. D'ya hear? Forget this, and you'll be all right."

I wish it were that simple. It's been seven years since Tewksbury, and still the memories creep up on me, seizing me with melancholy, restlessness, and despair if I'm not careful. I know Tim was right. I shall try to keep all this to myself and never tell the Kellers what I've come from. I shall be lonely, but I shall not be sorry I have come. The loneliness in my heart is an old acquaintance.

Chapter 3

Certainly this is a good time and a pleasant place
to begin my life-work.

—ANNE SULLIVAN TO SOPHIA HOPKINS, MARCH 1887

It's six thirty by the time I reach Tuscumbia. Sweltering in the southern heat, I watch the people come and go in their breezy spring clothes, and realize all at once how dowdy I must look. I step from the train and squint through the harsh sunlight at the faces about me. No one shows any interest in my arrival.

Finally a young man in a light suit catches my eye. As he looks me up and down, from my frumpy gray-and-red bonnet and burning eyes to my bedraggled dress and the felt bedroom slippers on my aching feet, the old shame of poverty darkens my cheeks. He looks almost as amused as the girls at Perkins did when I arrived from Tewksbury with neither nightgown nor toothbrush, unable to write my own name.

"Anne Sullivan?" He says no more, but I know from his tone that we shall never be friends.

"Annie," I tell him. My mild Irish lilt, so easy to hide in Boston, stands out like a gunshot among the soft-edged southern voices. The young man's eyebrow rises as though he fancies I've stepped off a boat straight from county Limerick.

He leans forward and takes my bag. "Mrs. Keller is in the carriage."

I follow him to the carriage, where a woman, not so much older than myself, waits. There's no sign of Helen. My anxiousness blooms into disappointment. How much longer until I see what's in store for me?

"Kate Keller," the young man announces with a careless sweep of his arm in my direction, "*Annie* Sullivan."

Mrs. Keller is tall and blond, with the kind of smooth skin I've seen only in the fashion plates Jimmie and I used to cut from the *Godey's Lady's Book* to paste on the walls of the dead house. She smiles—a warm smile, but a desperate one too.

"Oh, Miss Annie, it's so good to see you at last. Thank you so much for coming."

At the sound of her voice a great weight rolls from my heart. She speaks with such sweetness and refinement—as though her words come from the throat of a lily. I don't hesitate a moment when she extends her hand to help me into the carriage.

"Do you have any luggage?" she asks.

"I do. One trunk."

"James, go and see about Miss Sullivan's trunk."

"Yes, ma'am." His courtesy toward her seems to pain him. I watch him go, curious about Mrs. Keller's authority over him, for this James looks nearly twenty years old.

"Well, you can't accuse him of being too forward," I remark.

"James is my stepson, Miss Annie," she explains.

Leave it to Miss Spitfire, I think. It'll take a shoehorn to pry my foot from my mouth. I steal a glance at her face. It shows no trace of anything but kindness.

"Captain Keller's first wife died some years ago," Mrs. Keller continues.

Captain Keller. Holy Mother, I'd forgotten Helen's father fought with the rebels in the War Between the States. Dr. Howe would turn over in his grave if he knew a Perkins girl was working for someone who once owned slaves. I'd turn over in my own grave, if I had one.

I nod and try to smile through this newfound worry, but she takes no notice. "It's just wonderful to have you here." Again that hopeful smile. "We've met every train for two days."

Her friendly grace warms me like an arm round my shoulders. Before I know what I'm saying, I confess, "I think I've been on every train in creation in the last two days."

She laughs. "You'll feel better after a hot meal and a good night's sleep."

I hope to feel much better once I've met Helen, I

want to say. But I'd rather sever my tongue than risk being rude to this woman. Mr. Anagnos would marvel at my restraint if he could see me now—the girl who once threatened to scratch his eyes out.

James returns. "They'll deliver Miss Sullivan's trunk tomorrow," he announces, climbing into the driver's seat.

The words stumble out of my mouth before I have a chance to catch them. "Are we that close to—to home?"

"Only a mile, Miss Annie," Mrs. Keller tells me.

Excitement and anxiety roll in my stomach quicker than the turning of the carriage wheels as James drives us through the little town. The bright southern sun makes my eyes water, but the landscape helps quiet my restless thoughts. Tuscumbia looks more like a New England village than a town. Blossoming fruit trees line the roads and lanes—there are no streets—and the good, earthly smell of the ploughed fields floats on the air.

For a little while I can almost forget about Helen as the sights and smells of springtime melt away my memory of the gray Boston winter I left behind. Blooms lie draped over every bough like dainty shawls, and the green lawns glow in the early evening light. Modest redbuds and slender dogwoods texture the breeze itself with sweetness.

It shall not be hard to live in a place like this.

A nudge from Mrs. Keller interrupts my reverie.

Pointing down a long, narrow lane ahead of the carriage, she says, "Our house is at the end of there. We call it Ivy Green."

As the horse ambles round the corner, I can scarcely sit still in my seat. Finally the house comes into view, and it's all I can do to keep from jumping out of the carriage and pushing the slothful creature faster.

Chapter 4

Somehow I had expected to see a pale, delicate child—
I suppose I got the idea from Dr. Howe's description
of Laura Bridgman when she came to the Institution.
But there's nothing pale or delicate about Helen.

—Anne Sullivan to Sophia Hopkins, March 1887

Captain Keller waits in the yard for us. As the carriage pulls up alongside him, I see in an instant how James Keller will look twenty years from now, for they share the same strong face and smooth, even features. The captain's brown hair is quite thin on top, though, and his beard looks like a fistful of fine copper wires bristling down over his necktie. He fairly boils over with exuberance as he helps me from the carriage and pumps my whole arm up and down with his hearty handshake.

"Welcome to Ivy Green, Miss Sullivan," he booms.

I have to catch my breath to answer him. All that comes out is, "Where is Helen?"

He chuckles and takes my arm, leading me toward the house. I'm so eager to meet my little pupil I can hardly walk.

Stately magnolia and live oak trees anchor the lawn, curtaining the yard with their shade. Beyond them stands the house, plain and chaste as a cottage—not at all the grand plantation manor I'd expected. The walls are a crisp white, and the tall front windows have green shutters. An abundance of English ivy creeps all along the foundation and up the trunks of the trees.

Ten yards or so from the porch Captain Keller stops and pats my hand. "There she is," he says, nodding toward the doorway. "She's known all day that someone was expected, and she's been wild ever since her mother went to the station for you."

Helen stands on the porch, her cheek pressed against the railing's drapery of honeysuckle. Her chestnut hair is tangled, her pinafore soiled, and her black shoes tied with white strings. Her face is hard to describe. It's intelligent, but lacks mobility, or soul, or something. I see at a glance that she's blind. One eye is larger than the other, and protrudes noticeably. The familiar words ring in my ears before I can stop them: *She'd be pretty if it weren't for those eyes.*

But none of that matters. Something in me stirs when I see her, something that has lain still and cold since the day my brother died. She seems so utterly alone, her look so familiar, for a moment I imagine I'm seeing the shadow of my own child-soul. My arms ache to touch her, the desire so strong it startles me.

My foot is scarcely on the first step when Helen

races toward me with such force that I'm thrown backward against the captain. I right myself and try to take her into my arms, but she squirms from my caresses and writhes against my attempt to kiss her cheek, dissolving my sympathy into hurt.

Her hands roam everywhere at once—my face, my dress, my bag. Like a swift little pickpocket, she yanks the bag away from me and tries to open it. She struggles for a moment, then feels every inch of it. Finding the keyhole, she turns to me and twists one hand in the air like a key, pointing to the bag with the other. I'm delighted by her intelligence, in spite of this dismaying audacity.

"I'm sorry, Miss Annie," Mrs. Keller interrupts, her face pink. "Helen is used to our friends bringing sweets for her in their bags." She takes Helen's free hand and puts it against her cheek, shaking her head no so the child can feel it. Flushing to the roots of her hair, Helen purses her lips and jerks the bag closer to her side with a grunt. Short sounds, the same sort of noises that leaked from the throats of Tewksbury's insane, accompany Helen's every move. Mrs. Keller takes the bag by the handles and wrestles it away from her daughter—no meager feat, for Helen is large, strong, and ruddy, and as unrestrained in her movements as a young colt.

When the bag disappears from her reach, Helen's face contorts into such a theatrical pout that for an instant I want to laugh, but her outrage is so intense it's almost frightening. The Kellers, too, brace themselves for a storm.

Suddenly I realize what troubled me about Helen's appearance at first glance. Her features show none of the subtle ripples of thought and emotion that pass over normal faces. Only blunt reactions to pleasure or physical pain penetrate her vacant expression.

Desperate for a distraction, I dig in my pocket, wishing for the peppermints I ate on the train from Chattanooga. Instead I find my watch and put it in Helen's hand, wondering if I shall ever see it in one piece again. I show her how to open it, and instantly the tempest subsides. Helen takes me by the arm, and we go into the house and straight up the stairs together.

"Dr. Bell let her play with his watch in Washington, DC," Captain Keller muses from behind me. I wonder if he means Dr. Alexander Graham Bell. Either way, I take it as a compliment.

Upstairs I open my bag, and Helen rifles through it. Now and again she turns to me, bringing her hands to her mouth as though she's eating. She expects to find a treat, but I have no such thing; the doll from Perkins won't arrive until tomorrow. Reaching the bottom of the bag, frustration reddens her face.

Somehow I have to tell her that my trunk is on the way and there are good things for her inside. Such a simple thought. But how do I say it without words? How do I show her with no trunk and no treats?

Seized with an idea, I take Helen's hand and pull her into the slope-ceilinged sewing room off the hallway. With my hands over hers, I touch the large trunk standing in the corner, then point to myself and nod. She puzzles over this until I repeat her gesture for eating and nod again. Like a flash she dashes from the room.

I follow Helen halfway down the stairs and watch her make emphatic gestures to her mother. She seems to be showing Mrs. Keller that there is candy in my trunk for her. My chest begins to unknot. Helen's attempts to communicate are crude, but they make me hopeful that she can learn. Nodding, her mother shoos Helen back toward the steps.

With Helen's help I put my few things away. Her hands explore everything that comes from my bag. Nothing reaches its drawer without being touched and smelled, then modeled or paraded round the room. I can't help but laugh at the sight of her standing before the dresser mirror wearing my bonnet, cocking her head from side to side just as if she could see.

"Where did you ever learn that? You must be quite the little mimic."

While Helen amuses herself with my things, I look about our room. It's a large, comfortable room, with little in the way of knickknacks or decorations—probably more to do with Helen's roving hands than anything else. My bed stands behind the door, facing the window. On one side of the window is a fireplace with a narrow painted shelf boasting a handsome mantel clock and a pair of painted china vases. On the other is the dresser and the only other breakable objects in the room—a large washbowl and pitcher. Helen's little sleigh bed sits in front of the dresser, facing the door. Her playthings lay piled in a heap between the foot of her bed and the doorway. A school desk also has its place in that corner. A writing table with two rocking chairs sits before the window.

So this is what a child's room is supposed to look like, I think. What would Jimmie and I have done in a room like this, up to our knees in toys? Jimmie, who sneaked the scissors from the doctors' bags so we could make paper dolls out of the *Police Gazette*, and never complained when I snipped off their heads by mistake. When one of the doctors caught us, he shouted, "If either of you so much as looks at my instruments again, I'll slice off your ears!" But Jimmie only laughed and told me, "You're a better slicer with those scissors than any doctor, Annie."

Stooping down, I pull a small book from the pile Helen has cast aside. It's the little red dictionary Mrs. Hopkins gave me as a going-away gift. My spelling has always been atrocious. I would have liked a book of poems or Shakespeare better, to remind me of what I loved best at Perkins; the fastest friendships I made were within the lines of *Macbeth*, *King Lear*, and *The Tempest*. Though their words twine constantly through my thoughts, I'd relish the look of them on the page.

Still, the stoutness of this dictionary, its size and shape, please me. I run my fingers along the spine, savoring the feel of the leather. I lay it on the nightstand with a satisfying *thump*.

It almost looks like it belongs there.

I wish I felt the same.

Chapter 5

She is very quick-tempered and wilful, and nobody,
except her brother James, has attempted to control her.

—ANNE SULLIVAN TO SOPHIA HOPKINS, MARCH 1887

Next morning it takes me a moment to remember where I am. It seems I've overslept. Helen's bed lies empty, and there's not a sound in all the house. I wash and dress quickly, then go downstairs in search of company.

Alone, I explore the house. Mrs. Keller gave me a quick tour last night, but I was too tired to notice much more than my held-over supper plate and my bed. On the first floor are four square rooms, divided into pairs by a wide hall. The parlor and dining room lie to the left of the stairway, and two bedrooms to the right. The captain, Mrs. Keller, and baby Mildred sleep at the front of the house; the captain's spinster sister, Eveline, has the room at the back. Last night I discovered that James and his teenage brother, Simpson, share the upstairs room across from mine.

There's no sign of anyone about—not a breakfast dish or an unmade bed to be seen, so I wander out the back door into the sunshine.

Outside it's much more lively. Genial voices holler to one another in the carriage house, and chickens scuffle about the yard. Nearby, an old setter laps at a puddle under the pump. The light reflecting on the water needles my vision. More buildings are scattered about the property; the one next to the pump looks like a child-size Ivy Green. As I stand squinting with my hand shading my eyes, a boisterous racket claims my attention. Following the sound, I enter the small, barn-shaped kitchen.

The place is in an uproar. Through the yeasty dimness I spot Mrs. Keller, hunched over Helen, who sits at a flour-covered table pounding her fists and kicking her feet. A mound of bread dough trembles under the assault, and two patty pans bounce and jangle with every blow to the tabletop. A young Negro woman I assume is the cook has pressed herself into a far corner, her floury arms wrapped round a cowering colored child of about eight. The little girl clutches a limp piece of dough in one hand.

"What happened, Martha Washington?" Mrs. Keller cries over the clamor.

Wide eyed, the little girl answers, "We were just making our bread. She tried to tell me something with her hands, but I couldn't understand her quick enough."

In desperation Mrs. Keller's eyes sweep the room. When she sees me in the doorway, her face cascades through myriad emotions: surprise, embarrassment, then relief. "Miss Annie," she says, trying to sound calm and hospitable despite Helen's lashing fists, "would you please bring the butter churn to me?"

Confused, I look about. The churn stands beside me, its dash lolling out of the lid at a cockeyed angle. With a grunt I haul the full churn round the table to Mrs. Keller's side. In one darting move Mrs. Keller snatches one of Helen's hands and places the churn dash in it, moving the dash up and down, up and down, in a regular rhythm.

Quick as a summer storm, Helen's tantrum ends. She slides from her stool and takes up churning as though the devil himself were driving her. Gingerly little Martha and the cook resume their places at the table and begin working their dough.

Mrs. Keller gives me a weary look.

"I shouldn't have slept so late," I tell her. "I'm sorry."

"Nonsense," she says, straightening her dress and smoothing her hair into place. "You needed a good rest. Anyone could see that."

"That child's gonna make cheese outta that butter," the cook says to no one in particular.

"Oh!" Mrs. Keller cries, and whirls round. She tries to slow the rhythm of her daughter's churning, but Helen gives her a fierce shove and continues at her own wild pace. Sighing, Mrs. Keller wipes her hands on her apron, twisting the cloth round her fingers. "Are you hungry, Miss Annie? I had Viny save you a plate." Before I can sputter an answer, the cook has the plate in her hands, ready to whisk me off to the dining room.

"Oh, no, I can eat right here."

Viny freezes and glances at Mrs. Keller with raised eyebrows. I have a feeling no one has volunteered to eat in the kitchen before. "I don't want to be any trouble," I rush on. "I'd much rather sit with you and Helen." Viny looks unsure, but Mrs. Keller nods, and Viny makes a place for me between the coffee grinder and the apple corer. I take Helen's empty stool and plant it before my plate of biscuits, gravy, and eggs.

No sooner have the legs of the stool hit the floor than Helen appears at my side. I try to give her a good-morning hug, but she throws my arm from her shoulders. Instead she grabs a leg of the stool and pats her chest with her free hand. Her meaning–*Mine!*–is clear. When I don't budge, Helen bunches up her lips and thumps harder on her chest. Even in the dim kitchen light I can see Mrs. Keller's face turning pink again.

"Viny, get Helen some cake so Miss Annie can have some peace," she says. With a subtle roll of her eyes Viny complies and waves a hastily cut chunk of cake under Helen's nose. Like a vagabond, Helen snatches the cake and stuffs it into her mouth. Crumbs shower onto the table, a few of them lingering on her sticky mouth and chin. Some work their way into her tangled hair.

Her attention diverted, Helen sniffs about for anything else worth eating. Licking her lips, she hovers next to my plate of eggs.

The room halts.

I can feel everyone's eyes upon us. Suddenly Helen turns to the colored child and yanks at her dress, then stoops to the floor and doubles her hands like a ball. Martha says, "Awright, Helen," and out the door they scamper. A collective sigh of relief heaves all about me.

"What was all that?" I demand.

"Eggs," Viny says, turning back to her kneading.

"Eggs?"

"Helen likes to hunt for guinea hen eggs in the fields with Martha Washington," Mrs. Keller explains. "I'm sorry she was such a bother. She's been impossible all morning."

"Is that why her hair still isn't combed?" I say over a forkful of food.

Viny muffles a snort. Mrs. Keller stiffens. "A person can only fight so many battles, Miss Annie. I don't see the use of sparring over something she can't understand."

"There's a difference between understanding and simple obedience," I remark.

Mrs. Keller picks up the churn dash and begins to churn almost as fervently as Helen, but her voice sounds wistful as a wilting vine. "There was a time when Helen seemed to understand everything, Miss Annie. At six months old she could say 'how d'ye,' 'tea-tea-tea,' and 'wah-wah.' On her first birthday she took her first steps. She nearly ran across the room. And such sharp eyes! Why, she could find dropped needles, buttons, and pins before anyone else. Before that fever hit her, she was the brightest child I've ever known."

I'm intrigued. "And now?"

"She hasn't been sick a day since." She falters. Her melancholy smile fades. "I don't speak of it often. Living with it is enough. But I suppose you should know."

"Please."

"I don't know how much of Helen's mind is left," Mrs. Keller confesses. "She still says 'wah-wah' whenever she feels water, though I don't know if she realizes it. Everything we do, she follows with her hands, repeating every motion. She can sort and fold the laundry, and never makes a mistake. She feeds the chickens and turkeys, grinds coffee, and stirs the cake batter. One day I found her in the parlor with her father's glasses on, holding a newspaper in front of her face. Even things that don't make sense to her, she imitates." She stops short. I've cornered her, and she knows it.

"There's not much Helen can't do, provided she wants to do it," Mrs. Keller admits, "but she's so miserable I can't bear to punish her." She stops churning;

her grip on the dasher turns her knuckles white. "She wants so much to understand, Miss Annie. I've counted at least sixty signs she's invented for herself, but they're not enough anymore, as you saw this morning.

"Helen knows she's different. She touches people's faces as they talk, and I can see her wondering why her mouth doesn't work the same way. When she can't make us understand her, she moves her lips and gestures so frantically you'd think her little head was on fire with what she wants to say, but all she can do is scream herself into exhaustion."

"How often does it happen?"

"Every day. Sometimes every hour. We can't stand to see it anymore. My own brother says Helen behaves like she has no mind at all. He thinks we ought to lock her up somewhere."

My bones feel like hot wax at the thought of Helen in an institution—Tewksbury, southern style. "Do you believe that, Mrs. Keller?"

Mrs. Keller looks down at me with watery eyes, but her mouth goes hard with conviction. "No. She couldn't do all those things, or communicate at all, without a mind. Helen's still a bright child, Miss Annie. Isn't she?"

Searching for a bit of tact, I flick Helen's cake crumbs to the floor. "Well, she certainly knows how to get what she wants."

Chapter 6

The greatest problem I shall have to solve is how to discipline and control her without breaking her spirit.

—ANNE SULLIVAN TO SOPHIA HOPKINS, MARCH 1887

When my trunk arrives, I go out in search of Helen. I find her with Martha Washington on the kitchen steps, a mess of chickens and turkeys swarming thick as mosquitoes round their legs. Helen scatters their feed from a bowl in Martha's arms. Wading in among them, I try to catch Helen's hand, but she slaps me away and lunges for Martha.

The bowl tips.

Chicken feed rains down about our shoes. Helen's face darkens like a thunderhead as she feels the empty bowl.

"Uh-oh," Martha says, backing away. Even the chickens seem wary. Before Helen can make a fuss, I take her hand and point toward the house with it.

Helen shakes her head.

"She won't follow anybody anywhere," Martha tells me, "'less you give her a good reason.'"

"Is that so?" I snap, annoyed by Martha's knowing tone. When I came to Perkins, the little girls spoke to me that way. Big Annie, they called me when I was put to weaving mats with the kindergarten classes, though I was fourteen years old. I'd sooner eat chicken feed myself than be outdone by a spoiled six-year-old now. "She'll do what I say and nothing else," I declare, grabbing Helen's other wrist and holding tight, though she struggles almost hard enough to wrench my arms from their sockets.

After some vigorous jostling I see Martha's point—a bit of reasoning might not do any harm, provided I can jar Helen's attention.

Gripping her by the arms, I give Helen a good rough shake. Martha's mouth drops open at my harsh tactics, but I don't care. Judging from the little I've seen of her, the last thing Helen needs is another gentle hand.

My ploy works. Rattled but subdued, Helen appears to have forgotten the spilled feed. With her hands in mine, I trace the shape of a large rectangle in the air. She quiets. I make the trunk shape with her hands again and pat my chest. "Trunk, mine," I tell her, then point to the house. Quick as a monkey, Helen repeats my gestures. There's a fleeting moment of stillness, then her hands fly to her mouth. *Eat,* she mimes. A rapid succession of gestures follows: *Rectangle, eat, house.* A thrill runs down my spine as I interpret them. She remembers the treats I promised her yesterday!

I nod. Helen's face narrows, focusing with want. Kicking her way through the turkeys and chickens, she barrels down the steps in the direction I pointed. I dash after her, trying to lead her, but she flings my hand aside and lurches forward, arms outstretched and fingers splayed, groping through the air about her.

Once my trunk is open, Helen's hands prowl through my things like a pair of weasels. Nothing holds her attention for long; there is no fashion parade today. She dumps everything on the floor after a brief inspection, and it's all I can do to keep up with her as I stow each discarded item in the dresser.

Finally one of the doll's hands peeks out among the cloth. I hold my breath as Helen's fingers brush the cool porcelain. Her eyebrows crinkle for an instant, then she paws away the layer of skirts and shirtwaists and snatches the doll into her arms. Though she doesn't smile, a funny sort of delight shows on her face—more like satisfaction than pleasure.

I don't blame her; the doll is a blue-eyed beauty with smooth rosy cheeks, a mop of golden curls, and Laura Bridgman's fine lacework peeping out at the collar and cuffs of her delicate blue dress. A pang of jealousy stings my heart as I watch Helen mechanically rocking her new baby. Her plaything reminds me too well of the doll I discovered years ago among the Christmas gifts hidden in the parlor of Uncle John and Aunt Stasia's house. For weeks I coveted that doll, visiting her in every spare moment, longing for Christmas, when I was sure she'd be mine. But when Christmas came, my much-petted darling went to one of Aunt Stasia's little girls.

The doll in her arms, Helen scrambles over to me and pats first the doll, then herself with my hand.

It, me, is all the gestures say, but I fill in the blanks. *This mine?* she seems to be asking.

"Well, my little woman, this is as good a place to begin as any. Your first word will be 'doll.'" I take her hand, and instead of repeating her gestures, I form my fingers into the letter *d*. Helen's fingers spider over mine, exploring the shape I've made. When she seems satisfied, I make an *o*, then an *l*, then another *l*. This is the way Dr. Howe taught Laura, and the way I shall teach Helen. Every letter has a sign, every object a name. I point to the doll, point to Helen, then nod. *D-o-l-l, this, yours, yes.*

She blinks blankly and feels my hand, so I make the letters over again. *D-o-l-l.* I put my hand over hers and tap her fingers. *Your turn,* I'm telling her.

The letters come slowly but accurately; Helen's fingers curl in my hand like a small, warm shell. *D-o-l-l,* she spells, then points to it as I did. My heart wants to swell with pride, but I have to be cautious. To her, this could be little more than a game of monkey see, monkey do.

"Let's see if you can ask for it by name." I slip the doll out of her arms and try to spell the word into her hand. Her temper flares like a brushfire before I can form the first letter. In an instant Helen flies at me, kicking and swinging her fists. I catch one of her hands and try to bend her fingers into the letters, but she rakes the nails of her other hand over my face. Pain explodes against my eyelids.

"You devil!" I shriek. Ignoring my throbbing eyes, I tackle her, wrapping my arms round her waist. When Helen feels herself hoisted from the floor, she erupts into an extravagant tantrum, snapping and snarling like a wolverine.

Now what? I wonder, stranded in the middle of the room with a raging savage dangling from my arms. I'm tempted to dump Helen into my trunk and sit on the lid, but satisfying as that might be, it could cost me my job. And I can't expect Mr. Anagnos to find me another—he hardly knew what to do with me during summer holidays. On the other hand, if she takes another stab at my eyes, it might well be worth it.

Instead I heave her into one of the rocking chairs by the window and pin her down with my knee across her lap. Grabbing her hands, I cross her arms straitjacket-style over her chest. "I'd like to see you try that again," I growl into her face. Not about to be undone, Helen squirms and bucks under my weight so I can't keep the chair still, but I refuse to let her go.

Twenty minutes later I'm nearly exhausted, but Helen shows no sign of giving up—she has the temperament and tenacity of a sewer rat. Finally it occurs to me that she'll continue the struggle unless I do something to turn the current of her mind. The only thing I can think to do is bribe her with a piece of cake.

To distract her, I pull the rocker as far forward as it will come, then let go, flinging her back toward the wall as I bolt across the floor. The move buys me enough time to slip out the door and lock it behind me. From the hall I hear her wild cries of dismay as she barges through the room, searching for me and her doll, which I clutch against my heaving chest. Her voice sounds hollow and unfocused, as though even her throat is uncivilized. Shuddering, I head down the stairs.

The doll still in my arms, I burst into the kitchen. "I need a piece of cake!"

Viny gives me a queer look, which only fuels my impatience. "Supper'll be ready in an hour, Miss Annie," she says.

Brushing past her, I take the knife myself and carve out a large slab. "It's for Helen," I retort. "She's raising the roof in there." Cake in hand, I march out the door.

From the back of the house I hear Helen careening

through the room above. When I reach the bedroom door, I cross myself before turning the key. "Saint Christopher, protect her," I mutter, wiping at my running eyes, which still broil with pain.

Reluctantly as if I'm entering a lion's den, I open the door. Sensing the vibrations of my footsteps, Helen tears across the room toward me. For a terrifying moment I wish I had the wire mask and leather gloves Dr. Howe used against his fiercest deaf-blind pupil. I have only a slice of cake for protection.

Tossing the doll to the bed, I wave the cake under Helen's nose and fill her groping hand with the letters *c-a-k-e*. At the scent she turns wild with want, trying to climb my frame and reach the cake, but I hold it high over my head and pat her hand.

"Tell me what you want, little savage."

Her fingers flutter out the letters, and I hand over the cake. She crams it into her mouth, thinking, I suppose, that I might steal the treat away from her. When she's finished, I take the doll from the bed and graze its silky curls across Helen's cheek. Again she lunges for it but finds only my hand spelling *d-o-l-l* into hers. Grudgingly she spells *d-o-l*. I wait a moment, then slap the other *l* into her palm and relinquish the doll. Like a thief, she snatches the doll and runs from the room, smack into Mrs. Keller and her sewing basket.

As they collide, Mrs. Keller's hand drops over her daughter's. At her touch Helen's fingers jerk reflexively, spelling *d-o-l-l*, as pretty as you please. Mrs.

Keller stands thunderstruck, for the finger signs look identical to the letters they represent. The basket falls from her arm. "Miss Annie, what is this?" she gasps.

"Monkey chatter," I tell her, rubbing my forehead, which suddenly aches. "She doesn't have any idea what she's doing."

"But that was a word."

"No. It's nothing to her."

"She's holding the doll, Miss Annie. How can she not know?"

I sigh, searching for a way to explain it without disappointing her. "She's a parrot. I've taught her the letters, but she doesn't realize there's a link between them and the doll any more than a bird knows that 'Polly want a cracker' means, well, anything at all. A parrot only understands that mimicking the right noises produces a treat. There's no more to it than that."

Mrs. Keller frowns at my comparison. "Then what good are those letters?"

"If Helen can feel words, like this"–I take Mrs. Keller's hand and spell out the words as I speak–"the way a baby hears them day in and day out, one day she'll discover these letters are more than shapes. She'll realize signs have meaning, that they're symbols for the world around her."

"But what about the signs she's already invented? They're her own private language."

"I wish they were," I tell her, suppressing a

halfhearted laugh. "Her pantomimes are a mixed blessing–they show me her mind is alive, but they'll never be enough. What about the things she can't touch?" Mrs. Keller doesn't seem to grasp my meaning. "Imagine describing the difference between the taste of a peach and the taste of an apple with nothing but your hands."

She nods, and her arms encircle Helen. To my surprise, I feel a nip at my heart at the sight of Helen submitting so willingly to her mother's affection. "Her thoughts are trapped in her mind," Mrs. Keller says.

"They are," I tell her. "If you call a wordless sensation a thought."

I cup Mrs. Keller's troubled hand over mine and spell as I speak, hoping the shapes will soothe her. "But words, Mrs. Keller, words bridge the gaps between two minds. Words are a miracle."

Chapter 7

She is never still a moment.

—Anne Sullivan to Sophia Hopkins, March 1887

Fighting to fall asleep that night, I curse myself for speaking of miracles with Mrs. Keller. After what I saw at supper tonight, I'm afraid nothing will draw Helen's mind from its darkness.

Her table manners are appalling. Like a grazing animal, she wanders from plate to plate, plunging her hands into whatever takes her fancy. We may as well eat from a trough, the way Helen mingles our food together into mash.

Each of the Kellers handled Helen's foraging through their plate differently, telling me volumes about their attitude toward her. James did his best to maintain an air of cool indifference, though a few times I caught sight of him swiping her fingers out of his supper. Simpson enjoyed the commotion Helen caused, for it left his own sloppiness overlooked.

Although Helen never touched it, Mrs. Keller insisted on assembling a plate of the choicest morsels for her daughter, while the captain pressed on with business as usual, telling stories and pontificating on the glorious days of the Conferderacy as though nothing out of the ordinary were going on right under his nose. His sister, Miss Eveline, doted on Helen, petting the child like a kitten as she wandered by and feeding Helen from her own hands.

I hardly know which of them is worse.

The sight of Helen's dirty hands reaching for my food made me cringe. Foul memories of Tewksbury's own dining-room bully dredged themselves up inside me, the way scum surfaces on a bubbling pot of lye: Beefy, with his great, meaty hands—hands he often tried to put where they had no business when he was in charge of the women's eating hall. The meals he served looked just as appetizing as Helen's handiwork.

Mrs. Keller's cooking is pure magic, but between remembrances of Beefy and Helen's insistence on turning my supper to slop, I hardly swallowed a bite. I longed to fling her away, but under her parents' eyes I felt trapped between responsibility and obedience. Now, lying here miserable with heat and hunger, I'm fuming at the thought of letting her go unpunished.

I throw off the covers, stalk to the window, and brood, hoping to catch a bit of breeze. From a rocking chair I consider Helen, asleep in her bed. With her eyes closed and her limbs still at last, she could pass for a normal child.

But it's impossible to forget how different she may be. Not the deafness or blindness—her eyes and ears can't be the only doorways into her mind. It's the question of what lies behind those sealed doors that troubles me most. I can hardly bring myself to consider how blank it may be. At least I have the flutter of my thoughts to keep me company; in Helen's head is there anything at all, without even a voice to speak to herself? The idea leaves a tremor of panic in my throat.

I'm not sure I can do this job.

Yet a part of me understands Helen better than she does herself. I'm no stranger to frustration, anger, isolation. I wonder, though, how Helen can be content to deprive herself of my affection? The thought of her indifference makes my throat sting, yet I can't help feeling drawn to her. If I could only touch her heart, I know I could reach her mind. But she won't even let me hold her hand.

A small voice inside me cries, *I want to go home.*

Another answers, *What home?*

In the moonlight I catch a glimpse of Helen's new doll, tossed carelessly under her bed. Her golden curls are tangled, and it strikes my heart to see her suffer such callous treatment. I can't help but sneak alongside Helen's bed to pull the doll from her neglected corner.

I return to the rocking chair with the doll cradled in my arms and set to smoothing her hair, winding the soft ringlets round my fingers. Before I know it, my eyes grow hot as tears prick along their rims, and I'm crooning to Helen's doll like it's a baby. My thick throat burns, but the words of "Slievenamon" force their way out like air rising through water.

> Alone, all alone, by the wave-washed strand,
> All alone in the crowded hall.
> The hall it is gay and the waves they are grand,
> But my heart is not here at all.
> It flies far away, by night and by day,
> To the times and the joys that are gone. . . .

I wake next morning to Helen yanking the doll from my lap. For the first time, I'm glad she can't speak. I'd sooner die than let the Kellers know their daughter's governess spent half the night singing to a doll.

After breakfast I return upstairs to prepare another lesson for Helen. To my surprise, she arrives in the room soon after me, lugging a quilt behind her. She moves toward the vibrations of my footfalls and deposits the quilt at my feet. Tugging me to the floor, she touches my hand to the blanket, then to my chest.

It, you. Is that what she's saying?

I'm puzzled. Then Helen points to the bed, and I

remember asking Mrs. Keller for some lighter bedding this morning. How she convinced Helen to deliver it is more than I can fathom, but here Helen sits with the quilt between us and a saintly look upon her face. I'd like to reward her, but I don't have a crumb of cake.

Instead I pat her head like a puppy and spell *G-o-o-d g-i-r-l* into her hand.

G-o-o-d g-i-r-l, she spells back, patting her own head.

"What a fine monkey you'd make," I muse, next making sure she feels the cloth as I form the letters *q-u-i-l-t.* I tap her hand for her to repeat and she obliges, but her attention wanders elsewhere. Gathering the quilt into her arms, she blunders over to the bed and tries to strip back the heavy spread with her free hand. Amazed by her helpfulness, I cross to the opposite side of the bed and begin peeling off the covers.

The instant she feels me yanking at the bedspread, Helen dumps the blanket in a heap and scurries out of the room, slamming the door behind her. Blinking with surprise, I stand like a dressmaker's dummy, trying to make sense of her. Then I hear it.

Click.

She's locked me in.

My fury boils so high I can't move. "She's . . . locked . . . me . . . in," I growl through gritted teeth, one syllable at a time. Mad as a hornet, I hike up my skirt and clamber over the bed to the door.

"You beast!" I scream through the wood, hoping she can sense my anger in the force of my vibrating voice. Gleefully she rattles the handle, demonstrating her handiwork. I hope she's enjoying this stunt, for my pounding on the doorframe will be nothing compared with what she'll feel when I get my hands on her.

Outside I hear Mrs. Keller's feet hammering up the steps as fast as her wide skirts let her climb. "Miss Annie?" she calls, too sweetly for my taste. "Are you all right?"

I grip the molding on either side of the door, struggling to settle myself. We both know perfectly well what the answer will be.

"No."

"Is the door locked?"

I close my eyes and lick my lips. "It is."

"Helen took the key." This is not a question.

"She did."

Muffled scuffling sounds seep under the door, then more footsteps hustle down the stairs. "Miss Annie, she's . . . she's hidden the key."

"Is there no spare?" I spit out.

Hesitation. "No. I'll–I'll send for the captain."

I wonder if there really isn't a spare, or if Mrs. Keller realizes I'm likely to flay her daughter with my bare hands if she lets me loose. With nothing to do but wait, I drop into the rocker and heave myself back and forth until my legs ache.

Chapter 8

*I shall not attempt to conquer her by force alone; but I
shall insist on reasonable obedience from the start.*

—Anne Sullivan to Sophia Hopkins, March 1887

I've never been so humiliated in all my life. Bested by
a six-year-old and carried out the window and down a
ladder like a sack of Irish potatoes. I'd have stripped
the hide from that child if Mrs. Keller hadn't stepped
in to shield Helen from my wrath. I can't understand
the Kellers' permissiveness. I've learned from Mrs.
Keller that long before I arrived, Helen locked her into
the closet under the stairs, trapping her for a full three
hours. Mrs. Keller only sighs her long-suffering sigh,
but I'd have stuffed the little witch into that closet for
a week.

From the corner of the lawn where I sit nursing
my pride, I hear Captain Keller hefting my door from
its hinges. He insists on replacing the lock, though
heaven knows what for. No one in his right mind
will leave a key in a door again. I've single-handedly

rendered the entire Keller household unlockable. The disgrace of it makes my blood bubble, but I have to control myself. My smarting eyes can't bear another tantrum.

One thing is certain–Helen is no Laura Bridgman. It must have been different for Dr. Howe, who had a clingy, obedient pupil, driven by her teachers' approval. Given the right tools, Helen's willful, destructive nature could topple Western civilization.

It baffles me how a child unaware of even her own name could go about plotting to lock me in my room, complete with a quilt as bait. I shake my head at the wonder of it. There's no denying I'd enjoy Helen's mischievousness–if it weren't constantly making a fool of me.

The fact remains I can't afford another mistake like this. Two days' wages won't repay Mr. Anagnos for my train ticket to Tuscumbia, let alone the fare back. And the only way to prove Helen hasn't won is to behave as if her pranks have no effect on me. Today's lesson shall go on as planned.

Just as soon as the captain hangs my bedroom door.

I start with a peace offering–a sewing card.

It takes some doing to lure her back up the stairs to our room. When we arrive, she seems disappointed to discover the door handle turns freely once more. "I've had enough of that game," I tell her. "Try this one on for size."

She lets me lift her onto the bed and sit next to her. Holding the card over her lap, I begin sewing a length of woolen yarn through a line of holes, exaggerating my movements to entice her attention. As I expected, she follows my hands with hers: in and out, up and down.

Grabby and demanding as a toddler, she reaches for the card. For a moment I'm wary of giving her the needle. Even a dull kindergarten needle could become a fearsome weapon in Helen's hands. But unless I want this truce to end in a boxing match, I have no choice.

In a few minutes she's finished a neat line of stitches. She pats the card and pulls at my sleeve as though she expects me to praise her. "Apology accepted," I mutter, patting her head. *G-o-o-d g-i-r-l,* I spell. This time she pats my head with one hand while she repeats the words as a single fluid shape with the other; the individual letters mean nothing to her.

"Grand. Let's try another." I tap the card in her hand, spell *c-a-r-d*, then tap her hand.

C-a comes quickly enough, then she pauses. *Eat,* she mimes with one hand, pointing downstairs with the other. When I don't budge, she shoves me off the bed and toward the doorway. *C-a,* she spells again, then mimics eating.

"Cake!" I cry. "You remembered!" But her face is so vacant. Does she really remember anything beyond the shape of the letters? If the word meant anything to her, she'd have used it before. A child as fond of sweets as Helen would be trailing me with twitching fingers, begging for cake.

She seems to understand that *c-a-k-e* is related somehow to cake, but not that these movements in her hand can take the place of the object itself in her mind. If I want her to be more than a parrot, I need to show her that words have power.

"C-a-*k-e*," I explain, finishing the word with special emphasis on the last two letters. Dutifully as a servant, I rush down the stairs to fetch her some cake before the moment fades.

Helen delights in the success of her first primitive command, though I don't believe she recognizes it as such. She takes her time eating, as if my obedience has suddenly turned me into someone she can trust not to steal her treat away. Impatient to continue, I spell "doll" into her free hand and begin searching the room. As always, she follows my motions with her hands. When I reach her pile of playthings and begin to sift through her dolls, rejecting each one in turn, she points downstairs.

"D-o-l-l?" I spell out. Insistent, she points downstairs again. I can't be sure if it's my spelling or the dolls themselves that made her understand. "Well, go get it, then," I say, pushing her toward the door and using the same gestures she made when she wanted me to fetch the cake. Munching almost thoughtfully on her cake, she moves nearer the door, then stops, as if debating whether or not to go. Returning to my side, she gives me a shove and points downstairs.

"Think I'm your slave now, do you?" I spell "doll" once more, then repay the shove, shooing her to the doorway. "Get it yourself." Opening the door, I attempt to herd her outside, but she leans back into the force of my arms, refusing to move. "Which is it now, monkey or mule?" I mutter, grunting against her weight.

Giving up on force, I try another tactic: sabotage. With a sweep of my hand I snatch the half-gnawed cake from her grip.

Shock pours over her face, hardening it like a coat of varnish. I can almost feel the trust between us crumble. But I have to press on. Letting her smell the cake, I put her hand on my face and shake my head. *No cake,* I'm saying to her. I point downstairs. "Get the doll first."

She stands perfectly still for one long moment, her face crimson. Then her desire for the cake triumphs, and she runs out the door. Immediately I wish I'd spelled the words instead of using such a hodgepodge of pointing and gestures—then I might know which she understood.

With a sigh I collapse against the doorframe. My eyes are still hot and itchy from this morning's outburst.

When Helen returns, she exchanges the doll for the cake, then scrambles out of the room once more. "This will never do," I mutter to myself, and hurry after her.

Chapter 9

Her hands are in everything; but nothing holds
her attention for long.

—ANNE SULLIVAN TO SOPHIA HOPKINS, MARCH 1887

The afternoon turns into little more than a game of follow the leader. No amount of coaxing will convince Helen to return to our room. We've been up one side of Ivy Green and down the other, but nothing—not cake, dolls, nor sewing cards—attracts her interest. Instead she sits on the porch, stripping the leaves from the honeysuckle vine with cold precision.

This child is maddening. One word a day won't accomplish anything, and I can't keep her attention for more than a few minutes. Hauling her bodily up the stairs won't get me anywhere—we'll only end up having a wrestling match instead of a lesson. But I can't let her take charge. I'm the teacher, after all.

"And why should the learning stop because the lesson has ended?" I ask myself.

Yesterday I likened Helen to an infant. Perhaps

I should treat her as a baby instead of a student. I wouldn't force an infant to sit still until she learned to say "mama," would I? Of course not. Children simply absorb words as they go about their ways.

Very well. That's what I'll do with Helen. From this moment I'll be her shadow, feeding her words like milk from a bottle.

"L-e-a-f," I announce into her hand as she plucks another one from the vine. "Leaf. Porch. Railing. Vine." Everything within reach I name for her. I don't bother making her spell the words back to me. We'll practice later.

At first Helen seems interested. Her fingers follow mine. It becomes a game—she touches something, and it makes my fingers wiggle under hers.

Fence, gate, bench. Tree, shrub, hedge. Stone, dirt, grass.

We wander through the barn, carriage house, and kitchen, naming tools and animals, furniture and supplies. I begin to think she's waiting for something to stump me, something I won't move my hand in response to.

Soon my constant presence wears on her. She tries to avoid touching anything. But I'm persistent. Everything her hands fall upon as she gropes through the yard, I name. I'm sure she understands that the objects cause my movements, but there's no way of knowing if she realizes that the movements *name* the objects. But still, I spell. I spell until my fingers grow dull and clumsy, until the muscles between my wrist and elbow feel like frayed ropes.

At last the supper bell rings, and I surrender. Appeased by the sudden stillness of my fingers, Helen allows me to lead her into the house. As we near the dining room, Helen's nose comes alive, sniffing as though she's bent on tearing every scent from the air. But I march her past the dining room and the Kellers' bewildered faces, straight up the stairs to the wash-bowl on my dresser.

I can hear Captain Keller calling after me to come down for supper, but I pay no mind. If Helen's going to paw through my food, I'm at least going to see that it's with clean hands. As far as I can tell, she hasn't washed in at least two days, and her fingers have been in every-thing from the rose garden to the cow stalls this after-noon. Besides, I'd like to see the Kellers' faces when I present them with a well-scrubbed Helen.

"Miss Annie?" Mrs. Keller's voice drifts up the stairs behind me. "Are you all right?"

"Only a minute," I shout back.

I put Helen's hands on the pitcher and wait. Nothing. I dip my hand in the water and dribble a little over her fingers.

"Wah-wah." The syllables spurt from her hollow throat as automatically as a dog challenges an intruder. The wordlike sound shocks me for a moment, but Helen's blank face tells me it's nothing more than a lingering reaction, just as Mrs. Keller said.

W-a-t-e-r, I spell into one hand. She flicks the water at me and tries to back away.

"Think again, little witch," I tell her, pressing her between my body and the dresser. "You'll wash whether you like it or not." Clamping her hands against the pitcher, I force her to pick it up and pour the water into the bowl.

"Miss Sullivan? Miss Sullivan! Supper is on the table." The captain's voice is more substantial than his wife's, but I've no time to answer. Plunging Helen's hands into the water, I scrub for both of us. She does her squirming best to hinder my efforts, dousing me to the elbows. When the captain comes in, I'm having my revenge with a cake of soap and Helen's face.

"What is the meaning of this?" he thunders. Startled, I spin round. Helen twists away, still dripping, and flings her wet self into her father's arms.

I stand there, bewildered and blinking. "Meaning? There's no meaning. We're washing for supper."

He looks at my sodden shirtwaist, all the while stroking Helen's heaving back. "Are clean hands worth so many tears from an afflicted child?" His voice carries genuine distress. For a moment I wonder if the captain himself isn't about to cry.

My insides curdle. I don't know what to say.

Without a word he picks Helen up. She wraps her legs round his waist and buries her face into his shoulder. With a snap that makes me jump, Captain Keller yanks a hand towel from the dresser top.

"We've seen enough tears in this house," he mutters. In the doorway he turns, mopping Helen's face, and says, slowly and deliberately, "Supper is *served*, Miss Sullivan."

Rooted to the spot, I watch him go. The soap goes slimy in my hand. Here I thought they'd be pleased, and Captain Keller acts as though I've done nothing but rub salt in their wounds. My lips tremble. I don't know if it's because of the captain's harsh words or the sorrowful look in his eyes. Below me I can hear the scrape of the dining-room chairs on the floor as the Kellers nudge themselves up to the table. Then, an awkward silence.

They're waiting for me. I don't know if I can face them, red eyed and dripping, a failure once again. I'd much rather shrink into the rocker with Helen's doll. But if I want to keep my position, I have no choice.

Helen's beaten me again.

With a heavy sigh I press my eyes into the cool elbow of my damp sleeve, then head down the stairs.

Chapter 10

Her untaught, unsatisfied hands destroy
whatever they touch.

—ANNE SULLIVAN TO SOPHIA HOPKINS, MARCH 1887

The next day I rise early, determined to make some headway. Washing for supper may not have been enough to please them, but I'll dare the Kellers not to be impressed when they wake to find Helen dressed, combed, and washed.

First I dress myself and creep down to the kitchen. Viny is already preparing breakfast in the half-light. "I need cake," I tell her, "and plenty of it."

She gives me a dubious look. "You gonna spoil that child's appetite," she chides.

I fix her with a hard stare. "The last thing I intend to do is spoil that little bully," I inform her. "And as for her appetite, Helen's more likely to whistle 'Dixie' than refuse a bite to eat."

Viny laughs to herself and shakes her head. "You

sure right about that, Miss Annie," she says, heading for the platter. Her laughter makes me strangely confident. I smile as she hands over a generous plateful. "I'll bake another this afternoon." She winks. "You keep Missy Helen from cryin', and Cap'n won't give you a bit a trouble."

I cock my head and squint to make out her expression.

"I hear what I hear, is all," she replies, turning to her biscuit dough. "You really got her washed up yesterday?"

"I did."

"Humph," she grunts, "ain't that somethin'!"

I can't keep from grinning as I hurry back to my room. Helen is still asleep, so I set the cake on the floor between the dresser and her bed, then lay everything I need within reach. Dress and pinafore; stockings, high buttoned boots, and buttonhook; soap, brush, and towel. If I can wake her gently, I'm certain this will work. Perhaps by the end of the day I'll have won over more than Viny.

Kneeling beside her bed, I run my fingers over her hair. It's in dire need of a brushing but surprisingly soft. Delicate brown tendrils curl round her face. I could wind them into ringlets like the doll's, if she'd let me. The thought makes me smile. I lean in to kiss her cheek, and she stirs. One of my fingertips drags through a snarl of hair. With a jerk she sits upright, throwing her hands out to see what's disturbed her. She catches my hand, gives it a sniff, then snorts and tosses it aside.

"You're not so sweet-smelling yourself," I grumble, reaching for the cake with one hand and trying to hold her still with the other. She kicks free of the bedclothes and tries to scramble past me.

"Oh, no you don't." I spell *c-a-k-e* into her hand, then pop a morsel into her mouth. While she chews, I grab a stocking and hold it up for her to feel. "S-t-o-c-k-i-n-g," I tell her, then slip the end over her toes. She wriggles like a garter snake, but I don't give in until I have one leg covered, then the other. In between I placate her with more cake.

And so it goes. Before I put each item on her, I spell the name of it into her hand. At every step she resists, but if I keep feeding her, she stays reasonably quiet.

Until the boots. When she feels the leather, her patience breaks. As I'm spelling *b-o-o-t*, Helen launches the shoe into the corner, where it lands with a thud, scuffing the wall as it falls. Undaunted, I pick up the other boot and jam it onto her foot. Not about to be undone herself, Helen rolls across the floor, kicking, while I fetch the first boot. Then comes the buttonhook. She twists and claws at my face, forcing me to shut my eyes, but I wasn't half blind most of my life for nothing—I've been able to fasten a pair of high buttoned boots without looking since I was a wee thing.

Next I try heaving her over to the washbowl. But she refuses to stand. If I don't hold her upright, she collapses like a rag doll.

"So that's the way you want to do it?" I hiss at her. "Grand."

Leaving Helen where she lies, I lather up the little towel, then plant one foot on either side of her. "Think you've won, do you?" I drop a chunk of cake into her mouth to shush her. Before she can consider sitting up, I kneel over her, straddling her so my weight pins her to the floor. In two swift moves I grab each of her hands and wedge them between my knees and her sides.

"Make a fool of me, will you," I pant, and scrub until her face gleams pink from the rubbing, then red from her temper. She flails, grunts, and sputters. Her bellowing cry, "Wah-wah," sends cake crumbs flying into my face and her hair, but I don't care—her hair is next on my list, and washing my own face will be a joy after this.

W-a-s-h, I spell with deep satisfaction when I free her hands and scrub them, too. I can hardly wait to see the Kellers' faces when they see their girl shined up like a new penny.

Her hair is another matter entirely. I can't very well run a brush through it while she's lying down.

After some grappling we end up sitting one in front of the other, my legs wrapped round her waist. I clamp a hand over her mouth and chin to keep her from howling, then set to work with the brush.

It's tedious work. Even with my legs restraining her, Helen thrashes so it's impossible for me to do anything but tear the brush through her hair. A sickening rip accompanies each stroke. In the end I make a concession: Any more brushing and Helen's tearful morning will be impossible to hide from the captain. Already I hear stirrings in the rooms below me.

Satisfied as I'm going to be, I turn Helen loose. She fairly rockets down the stairs. Paying her no mind, I tend to my rumpled hair and dress. Before I leave the room, I glance to where the Perkins doll sits propped against my pillow, smiling her coy china smile. I grin back. "She looks as lovely as you now, doesn't she, dear heart? Won't Captain and Mrs. Keller be pleased?"

When I reach the dining room, my smile fades. The place is in shambles. Amid the fragments of a large serving dish Helen sits stuffing her face with scrambled eggs. Mrs. Keller stands beside an upturned chair, holding baby Mildred high at her shoulder, while the captain rubs at his shin, wincing. Simpson is wide eyed; James, frosty as ever.

My heart sinks. I hardly need ask what's happened. None of their eyes accuse me, but I know. This is all my fault. The quiet is horrible, but Viny's voice is somehow worse when she speaks, for I know that she knows too.

"Give the baby here, Miss Kate," she says, turning the chair over for Mrs. Keller. "I'll put her down to rock."

"Viny–," Captain Keller begins, but she cuts him off, nodding.

"Yessir, Cap'n, I know. More eggs. But somebody'd better sweep up that broken china before Missy Helen cuts her fingers to ribbons," she says.

Grateful for something to do, I drop to my knees and fish through the mess for bits of the broken dish. "You go on," I tell Viny. "I'll take care of this."

Mrs. Keller sighs and sits down. "That was my last serving bowl from this set," she murmurs.

"The pieces are large, Mrs. Keller," I offer. "Perhaps a little glue?"

That same tired smile appears. "No, Miss Annie. It's too far gone. Some things just aren't worth the trouble it takes to bring them back."

Tears prickle at my eyes. I turn back to the floor to hide my face. I wanted so much to please them. I worked so hard, and for what? Even if they noticed how fine I had Helen looking, they'll never remember after this.

I can hardly look at them. The words sizzle in my head, and I want to shout at them, *If Helen were a seeing child, you'd expect me to turn her over my knee for the trouble she's caused!*

But how can I? With Mrs. Keller looking as broken as her china bowl, and the captain ready to present me with a one-way ticket to Boston if I lay a hand on his poor little girl, how can I afford to give Helen even a taste of the discipline she needs? It seems nothing I do comes out right.

But in my heart I know what's right for Helen: obedience, love, and language. Come what may and hell to pay, I'll find a way to give her all three.

Chapter 11

She was very troublesome . . . this morning.

—Anne Sullivan to Sophia Hopkins, March 1887

I start with obedience.

After dinner I gather a few objects for a lesson and arrange them at the table in front of the window upstairs. In spite of yesterday's fiasco I'm not willing to give up on regular lessons yet. A schedule–and with it, structure–shall be Helen's first step toward obedience. Still, I'm going to start small: "doll," "beads," and "card" are enough for today. If nothing else, I intend to teach her who's in charge.

Armed with a bit of cake, I go downstairs to fetch Helen. I find her in the parlor, rocking a much-abused rag doll in little Mildred's cradle. She moves the cradle with the same fervor she showed the butter churn two mornings ago. If the poor doll had a brain, it'd be addled into cottage cheese by now. Thinking to appease her, I put the hunk of cake into Helen's right hand and grasp her left one to lead her up the steps.

God above! You'd think I'd tried to drag her up by her toes, the way she fusses—clawing, kicking, and finally going limp and dangling by an arm.

"That's enough of that," I growl, releasing her hand. She drops like a sack of coal and scuttles back to the parlor. Hot on her heels, I follow and grab her by the arm. She twists and gropes for anything—cradle, doorframe, banister—to brace herself against, but it does her no good. When we reach the stairs, I stop only long enough to hoist her up under my arm, balance her against my hip like an upturned baby, and haul her up the steps.

I plunk her, panting, into the chair and spell *s-i-t*. I tap her hand, but she refuses to repeat the word back to me. More to my surprise, after her tussle over the trip upstairs, she doesn't move at all.

"Is it the silent treatment, then?" The absurdity of the question hits me, and I laugh aloud. "Be a silent witch if you want. I can do the talking for both of us." I suppose it's every bit as absurd of me to speak aloud to her. Ridiculous or not, I can't see the use in muzzling myself for hours on end simply because she can't hear. Besides, I've never been inclined toward holding my tongue.

Guiding her movements, I make Helen feel the doll with one hand as I try to spell the word into the other. She yanks her closed fist away, shoving it into her lap.

I slap my own hand over her clenched fingers and pull her arm toward me.

I hear the sound before I understand what's happening.

Thwack!

The table topples onto its side, spilling my lesson over the floor. Helen's booted foot swings gaily in the space where the table stood. As usual, she doesn't smile, but a hint of smugness plays across her face. I don't care for it in the least. *I will if I want to, and I won't if I don't,* that look says—the very thing I said to the first teacher who tried to command me.

I give her a wry half smile as my hand lands on her ankle with a *snap*. "If I didn't know better, I'd think my teachers had sent you to avenge them," I tell her, stilling her boot and resisting the temptation to squeeze until I hear the shoe leather creak. "Think you can get the better of me, do you? Not today, my little spitfire. Not today." She squirms against the pressure of my grip. After a moment I release her.

I right the table and replace all the objects. Helen reaches out for an instant to feel the table, then crosses her arms in a sulk.

"That's right, you. There's no stopping me today." I reach into the crook of her elbow, grabbing for one of her hands. She hunches up like a turtle, clamping them up under her armpits. Her resistance only stokes my resolve.

Crouching on my knees beside the chair, I lunge in with both hands to wrestle one of her arms free. She grunts like a bull, clutching her hands to her sides. Suddenly all her defiance falls away, and I hold one wrist in my hand like a trophy. I don't realize my mistake.

Her other fist flies like lightning. I hear a *crack* inside my head and think for a moment of thunder, until something in my mouth distracts me. Something small and cool as the hand of a china doll.

A tooth. *My* tooth!

I slap a hand over my mouth and hold my breath, waiting for the pain. There is none. Only a slow-waking ache in my jaw. I open my mouth and gasp for a breath.

Searing cold slices across the broken tooth's edge. Tears boil up in my eyes, and my throat swells, but I can't cry, for fear of the scalding pain. I press both palms to my mouth and try to breathe slowly through my nose. Brassy-tasting blood runs from a split inside my lip.

I stumble toward Helen, and she scrambles away, warned by the clumsy jolts of my feet. "Come back here, you beast!" I cry after her. The exposed tooth-stump throbs with every word. A sob breaks out of my chest, slowing me for an instant as I stagger out of the room and stampede, moaning with each step, down the stairs.

I'll demolish that child. No one has hit me since I

learned to fight my own father, and I'm not about to let anyone start.

I wheel round the banister, hell-bent on getting my hands on Helen. Drawn by the pounding of my feet, Mrs. Keller appears in the parlor doorway, her face a question. "Miss Annie?"

"Where is she?" I snarl through the fist pressed against my mouth.

Her glance darts toward the back door, but the fire in my eyes keeps her from answering. "What is it?" she asks. Her composure amazes me.

"Where is Helen?"

My tone puts her on guard. "Miss Annie, what is it?"

"What is it? I'll show you exactly what it is!" With a wincing flourish I spit a messy gob of tooth and blood into my hand and thrust my palm under her nose. "There! Your lovely little girl did that to me. Now, where is she?"

Mrs. Keller pales. "Miss Annie, please. You must consider . . ." She hesitates a moment, uneasy at the force of my anger. "Helen doesn't know any better."

"That won't be so when I'm done with her."

My threat makes her lips stiffen. "It's hardly fair to punish her for something she doesn't understand." She lays a hand over the newel post, subtly blocking my path to the door. The poise I admire so much in her suddenly infuriates me.

"You want to talk about fair when I'm standing

here with a mouthful of blood and a gap in my jaw? I'll tell you something, Mrs. Keller, there'll be no 'fair' in this house while that she-devil runs loose!"

Her eyes lower for an instant, but her body doesn't budge. "I'll have Viny bring in some ice and rags for your mouth," she says, meeting my gaze at last. Frost tinges her blue eyes; the corners of her mouth waver.

I shudder as my fists clench, digging the broken tooth into my palm. My voice rasps, "I'll be in my room."

She looks me over once more, then turns and hurries down the hall toward the back door. Once, she sends a nervous glance over her shoulder. I haven't moved an inch, though my fist grips tighter and tighter round my ruined tooth, until I think my knuckles will burst open. When the door shuts at last, I scream and fling the bloody handful down the hall behind her.

The sound rips through my jaw, leaving me in a panting heap on the bottom step. All I can do is sit with my hand cupped over my lips, sucking cool air through my nose to warm in my lungs before I let it touch my throbbing mouth. The feeling is as raw as my memories.

* * *

The lamp gutters low, and my mother moans in the bed. My brothers and sisters are asleep, but in the next room I hear voices, their edges dulled by drink. My father's is one of them. Roused by the wavering melody,

I grope my way out of bed. Inside the doorway I stop in surprise when my hands blunder into a feathered lump hanging from the wall. My fingers find a fanned tail and scaly claws—a turkey! Around the table I make out the shapes of four men, joking and singing to the tune of "Seven Drunken Nights." I hear the slap of cards on the table, and I know they're gambling. Up to the table I go, determined that my father should win. I put out my hand to touch one of the cards, and someone slaps it away. My temper flares, but another hairy hand pats mine, lingering a moment too long. Someone sniggers across the table, and I yank my fingers out from under the heavy paw. I scurry back to my mother's bedside, but she's too ill even to toss or turn.

The night wears on and the lamp flickers lower. Before long the men are guffawing and making up their own verses to the song. In the bed my mother whimpers and cries softly as their language grows more powerful and the house begins to rattle with the stomping of their feet. "Annie," she whispers, "ask them to go. Please."

Back in the next room, I creep to my father's elbow. "Dad, Mam says would the men please go home." My father's hand explodes across my cheek, and the group lets out a raucous laugh. One of the men sways up from his chair and falls to the floor. *I hope he dies*, I fume to myself, but he wobbles to his feet, pulls the turkey from the wall, and staggers out the door. Away they stumble, one by one, and I hear them calling,

"Merry Christmas!" through the icy wind. At last the lamp goes out, and I vow no one will hit me again.

* * *

With a sigh I turn and climb the stairs, leaning heavily on the rail. When I'm nearly to the top, the light fixture mounted on the ceiling of the hall catches my eye. Up close like this I can see for the first time a design frosted into the glass globe. Leaning over the rail, I squint, and my straining eyes widen in disbelief.

Plump children frolic among the trees etched into its surface. One of them is blindfolded.

Blindman's bluff.

I don't know whether to laugh or cry. In this house, of all places, a game of blindman's bluff carved into the light itself.

Chapter 12

*Although I try very hard not to force issues, I find it
very difficult to avoid them.*

—ANNE SULLIVAN TO SOPHIA HOPKINS, MARCH 1887

I feel their eyes on me when I arrive at breakfast next
morning. I don't like it. The day feels strange enough
already. As soon as I woke, something in my room
felt different. When I looked about, I saw Helen's
bed hadn't been slept in. It was easy to guess she'd
spent the night downstairs with her parents. A harder
question is why. I doubt Helen had any choice in the
matter. I'd like to think the Kellers kept her away out
of courtesy, to let me recuperate undisturbed, but
seeing their faces round the table, I'm sure the truth
is different.

Maybe they were afraid—afraid of me. The idea
makes the swarm of hunger in my stomach sour into
dread. Do Helen's parents really think I'd hurt her?
What do you expect them to think, I sputter to myself,

after you stood there with a fistful of gore, baying for blood?

I nod good morning and take my place at the table. Helen, rumpled and tousled as ever, sits alongside her mother. Avoiding the sight of her, I turn my attention to breakfast. The white tablecloth is so bright it stabs at my sore eyes, but the smell of the food overpowers my unsavory thoughts. There is sausage and eggs, fresh bread, canned sliced fruit, and Mrs. Keller's delectable homemade preserves. The coffee, piping hot, is already poured, and a frothy pitcher of fresh milk stands ready.

Helen begins to squirm before Captain Keller finishes the blessing. This I overlook. Soon, though, I can't help notice every platter of food passes by Mrs. Keller and Helen before it comes to me. Helen gets first pick of every dish. I might tolerate this if she actually ate the food on her plate. Instead Helen begins to wander like a stray animal from chair to chair, dipping her hands into whatever pleases her. She has no limits: plates, serving dishes—even the sugar bowl, the butter dish, and the jars of honey and preserves are fair game. For a while she settles in with a pot of blackberry jam, scooping out great fingerfuls, then slurping away like a bear at a honey tree. The sound makes me cringe.

When she's had her fill of jam, Helen circles the table again, sampling from each plate. Blackberry seeds dot the bruise-colored stains on her fingers. Soon she's greasy with sausage from Miss Eveline's plate and dripping with gooey syrup from her father's sliced pears. At Simpson's place she swipes her hand over his slice of bread, smearing away a layer of honey and crumbs.

My plate comes next.

As I watch her filthy hands grope toward me, trailing a path of muck along the tablecloth, the ghost of a Tewksbury voice hisses in my ears. *Beggars, thieves, whores, and what do you expect?*

Beefy.

I can't stomach the thought of Helen's hands in my breakfast any more than I could stand Beefy's misshapen fingers anywhere near me while I choked down his intolerable food. Soggy bread and rancid butter. Eternal corned beef and gray, lumpy stew. My plate will look no better than Beefy's cooking when Helen finishes with it.

Her hand darts in front of me and lands–*smack!*–in my mound of eggs. Like a spider drawing up its legs, she pulls her fingers into a fist, dragging a pile of food into her grasp. The yellow bits slither out between her knuckles.

I stare at the hand-shaped hole in my plate, and the anger dances along my spine. Do they really believe I'll swallow this, too? *What do you expect?* Beefy howls in my head. *Broiled chicken and lobster, I suppose, and cream cheese from the dairy of heaven!*

But this isn't Tewksbury. I'm an employee here, not a beggar, nor any other class of degenerate. Grasping my fork with a trembling hand, I cut away every trace of the eggs Helen touched, and shove the desecrated pile to the edge of my plate.

Before she rounds the table again, I set my arms alongside my plate like a schoolgirl blocking a nosy desk mate. When Helen feels my arms in her way, her eyebrows scrunch together. She tries to reach beside me, over me, under me. I block her each time. Perturbed, she scoots past, heading for her mother's unguarded dish. I look about. Only Simpson has noticed my defense. He watches me with a glint in his eye, as if he senses excitement to come.

Once round the table Helen goes, gathering more greasy crumbs. My concentration on her distorts the Kellers' oblivious conversation into goose chatter. The closer she steps, the more violent her movements become. Something's agitated her. Only Simpson and I know what it is.

As she approaches, I feel I'm being stalked. The family may act as if Helen is a beloved pet fit for spoiling and indulgence, but I see through them. She's no better than a wolf, feeding on their fear.

But I've survived too much to be afraid of anything a six-year-old might do to me.

I catch her hand in midair and place it on the table. She moves to my other side and reaches again. I put her hand on her own plate. She rushes at me, trying to bowl me out of my chair, but I brace myself and meet her charge. Again I grab her hands and slap them down onto her plate. She grunts and whirls on me, both hands upraised.

Mrs. Keller rises and starts for Helen. Her face wears that soft, shameful look, and I know she'll do nothing but take Helen aside and ply her with cake if I give her the chance.

"No!" I cry over Helen's grunts. Across the table, Miss Eveline gasps at my impudence. A low whistle sounds. I look up and see James, eyebrows raised, and something like a smile on his face. Narrowing my eyes, I sneer back at him, flashing the gap in my jaw. Dodging her fists, I grab Helen by the arms and grapple with her.

"Miss Sullivan," the captain's voice warns as Helen begins to howl. "I don't care what you do in Boston, this is not how we treat children in this house."

Beefy's final shout in my brain echoes Captain Keller's sentiment: *One more word and I'll throw you out!*

"When this beast starts acting like a child, I'll be happy to change my ways," I retort, defying both of them. Simpson hoots with laughter, clapping a hand over his mouth. Captain Keller fixes him with a freezing look. "Let her walk all over you if you like, but I'll have no more of this," I shout over Helen's caterwauling.

"I shall not permit anyone to raise a hand to my daughter, Miss Sullivan," the captain declares.

"Indeed! You'd sooner see your family and your guests cower like beaten dogs before her."

"She's only six, Miss Annie," Mrs. Keller implores, "surely you don't expect–"

"Are you going to tell me you expect her to up and turn civilized at twelve? Eighteen? Twenty?" I look wildly from one end of the table to the other. Neither of them answers. "If you don't stop her now, it's a prizefighter you'll be hiring to cope with her later."

Making use of my distraction, Helen flings herself to the floor, flailing her arms and legs like an upturned beetle. Captain Keller stares at her for a long moment before his chin quivers and he strides out of the room.

Mrs. Keller stands poised between her husband and me. Pain twists her lips. Her gaze follows the captain out the door behind her, then moves to Helen. Tears gloss her eyes as she turns them up at me.

My voice is little more than a whisper. "I won't hurt her, Mrs. Keller."

Her mouth sags. She draws a breath and nods. "Boys," she says to James and Simpson, and goes out. The brothers follow her. Last of all Miss Eveline rises to leave. At the sideboard she pauses, then pulls a key from the drawer.

"You stay sharp, now, dear," she says solemnly, placing the key in my hand. The concern in her voice closes my throat. "Our Helen is smarter than all those other Kellers put together."

I nod, then lock the door behind her.

Chapter 13

I had a battle royal with Helen this morning.

—Anne Sullivan to Sophia Hopkins, March 1887

Helen kicks and screams for a full half hour after her parents desert the table. It's almost more than I can bear. Her otherworldly sounds are strangely, horribly familiar. How many nights did those same sounds lull me to sleep at Tewksbury? Only, in the almshouse it was the feebleminded patients that made them. Long into the night they'd yowl and cry without meaning to, their minds too weak to control even the thin muscles of their throats.

Half an hour I struggle to ignore Helen and eat my breakfast. The food almost chokes me. I'm stinging with hunger, but my sore mouth aches, and Helen's racket sets every nerve in my body to jangling. I'd dearly love to pin her down and stuff her face with a napkin, but I refuse to fuel her tantrum with any sort of attention.

As if the screaming isn't enough, the little witch tries at odd moments to yank my chair out from under me. If I don't hold myself rooted to the spot, I'm likely to pounce on Helen and tear the screaming mouth from her face.

Finally, finally, her war whoops cease, and she crawls up the side of my chair to see what I'm doing. She gropes her way along my arm to my fork, then stops. I brace myself as Helen reaches for my cheek, but she only wants to feel my jaw as I chew.

She reaches for my plate. I brush her hand aside. She stamps a foot and reaches again. I shove her back with a dismissing wave. She moves to the other side of me and reaches once more. I block her with an elbow in her chest. Her little lips purse like a dried-up rosebud, and her face goes red.

Her hand darts to my arm and pinches a tiny bit of flesh between her fingertips, clamping tighter than a sparrow's beak. It's as if she's arrowing all her pent-up frustration into my skin. Before I can gasp from the pain, my hand shoots out and strikes her full on the cheek.

Startled, Helen blinks and releases me, only to dive in a second later with both hands.

I slap her harder.

She twists my skin between her fingers, grinding the flesh until I can feel the bones beneath the pads of her fingers. I cry out, smacking her again. The sound rings through the room. I sit frozen, waiting for the Kellers to appear.

Nothing happens.

Helen retreats and returns to her circuit round the table. At her mother's place she gropes about the plate. Finding no familiar hands, she searches the empty chair for Mrs. Keller. A bewildered look falls across her—I think it's the first expression besides greed or anger I've seen on her face all week. Baffled, she moves to James's place, then Miss Eveline's, Captain Keller's, and Simpson's, growing more frantic as she goes.

Reaching me again, she jerks away with a snort. For a moment she stands still, working her mouth like a ruminating cow. Then she slinks to her plate and crawls up onto her chair.

"Well, look at you," I muse as she begins eating her own food with her fingers. "If you weren't so charming, you could pass for a lady." Without silverware, eating with her fingers is the best Helen can do. "But you can do better, I think," I tell her. Leaning over, I press my spoon—no knives or forks for this wild one— into her hand.

The spoon clatters to the floor. Defiant, Helen lowers her chin to her plate and shovels the food toward her mouth.

Her insolence propels me like a whip from my chair. Grabbing her hand, I point with it to the floor, indicating the spoon. "Pick that up," I bark. She writhes beneath my grip, stretching for her plate. With a sweep of my arm I shove the food out of her reach. She tries to shimmy over the table toward it, but I catch her pinafore ties and haul her back. "Nothing for you until you pick up that spoon," I repeat, pointing her hand toward it with each word.

The whole of her body seems to dig into the chair.

Moving to her back, I try to pull Helen's seat away from the table, but she clings to the tabletop, linens and all. The entire table setting inches toward me as I edge Helen and the chair backward. Tipping the seat toward the floor, I try to dump her in a heap, but she wraps her legs round the rungs and dangles between table and floor.

Panting, I abandon the chair and go straight for her body. With my foot braced against the seat of the chair, I wrap my arms round her waist and pry her from the table. The china quivers as she loses her grip on the tablecloth.

Dislodged from her stronghold, Helen thrashes like a broken-winged bird, so I'm forced to drag her across the room toward the spoon. When I nudge her boot against it, she refuses to bend and pick it up. It doesn't matter–I fold her up and shove her to the floor as though she's nothing more than a stubborn jack-in-the-box. I put the spoon in her hand, but she refuses to hold it. She flails and squirms, thrusting her hands into my face and digging her nails into my scalp.

Huffing with exertion, I wrestle the spoon into

Helen's hand, clamp my own fist over hers, and yank her to her feet. Back to the table we limp. At every step she locks her knees like a stubborn billy goat, and I kick at the backs of her legs with my own knees to prod her ahead. All the while I keep my hand locked over hers, for she writhes as though I'm making her carry a fistful of fire across the room.

At the table I jam Helen down into her seat and shove her chair forward until it pinches her against the table. Still holding the spoon in her hand, I scoop eggs from her plate and try to guide the spoonful to her mouth. Her arm turns stiff as a railroad tie, and she presses her lips together tighter than a stack of folded newspapers.

"Think you can outlast me?" I move behind her and wrap my arm round her chest, locking her left arm to her side. Cheek to cheek, I brace my head against hers to keep her from jerking her neck aside.

"Got you in my arms at last," I mutter in her dead ear as I inch our clasped right hands toward her mouth. Before I'm done, I have to press the spoon against her lips until they turn white to make her open up. At last my size and strength prevail, and I compel her to take up the food with the spoon. After a few bites she yields and I release her.

Perched on the tabletop, I watch her eat like a human being. *Wait until the Kellers see this,* I gloat to myself. One victory, at last.

Or so I think.

Chapter 14

It was another hour before I succeeded in getting her napkin folded.

—Anne Sullivan to Sophia Hopkins, March 1887

When Helen's cleaned her plate, she flings the napkin to the floor and runs to the door. Finding it locked, she kicks and screams all over again.

"Lord above," I groan, pressing my fingertips to my temples. Minutes pass. An aching pulse behind my eyes throbs to the beat of her fearful racket. Driven by the pain, I stride to the door, grab Helen by the shoulders, and shake her until her teeth rattle. "Enough!" I shout at her. "If you won't leave this table like a civilized person, you can spend the night here."

I wrench her back to the table and push her to the floor. Slapping her hand over the crumpled napkin I thunder, "Pick it up." She sits still, pouting. I wiggle her hand over the napkin again. Nothing.

"Fine!" I yank the napkin out from under her hand and whip it into her lap. With a grunt and a groan I scoop Helen up, napkin and all, and deposit her into the chair.

The sudden relocation stuns her; she quiets. Kneeling beside her, I fold my own napkin and lay it on the table next to hers. Taking control of her hands, I let her feel the rumpled napkin and my head shaking no. Then I move to the folded specimen as I nod yes.

I pull up a chair beside her and demonstrate the proper way to end a meal: fold the napkin and place it on the table. If she can sort and fold laundry, there's no excuse for her not to crease a bit of cloth into a square before leaving the table.

My show of etiquette does not impress her. When I lay Helen's napkin over her lap, she dumps it on the floor with a flick of her wrist. I lean over and retrieve it, snapping it back into her lap. "You can have that one for nothing. Try it again and you'll be sorry." Without a hint of hesitation she pitches the napkin from her lap. I spring from my seat and topple Helen from her roost with a deft twist of her chair. She sprawls on the floor, too surprised to yowl. I can't help but laugh–despite her own savagery, sparring with someone as fierce as she shocks her.

I don't laugh for long. She digs at my legs with her sharp little claws, making me think I've blundered into a colony of fire ants. I kick at her until she crawls under the table. She doesn't budge until I get down on my hands and knees and come after her. Even then she scrabbles just out of my reach, until I drag her back out by her hem.

At last she climbs onto her chair, leaving the napkin behind. Exasperated, I send her sprawling again, and the battle begins anew. Every time she sits down without the napkin, I throw her out of her seat. Every time I throw her out of her seat, she attacks me and retreats under the table. By the time Helen finally surrenders, trailing the napkin behind her like a white flag, holes pock my stockings, and her dress hangs ragged as a Tewksbury beggar's.

We have another tussle over folding her napkin.

I know she knows what to do with it. But she only sits, still and solid as a mule. Her face goes rigid. I'm wary. This is the sort of pose Helen took before she broke my tooth. Standing behind her, I try to move her hands through the motions of folding. Playing patty-cake with a tin soldier would be easier. She holds her arms stiff as planks, letting her hands come ever so close, but never near enough to shape the folds. As I fight with her, the muscles in my arms shudder, betraying my fury.

An idea leaps to my mind like a spitting ember. I grab my own folded napkin and clap it over Helen's mouth and nose. My promise to Mrs. Keller flashes through my mind, but I lay it aside. Unless I actually smother Helen, I won't be hurting her.

As Helen kicks at the air, I pull her head back and anchor it against my torso. Grasping a flailing hand, I touch it to the napkin in her lap. She tries to twist her body away from me but can't escape my grip on her chin.

I count to forty, then give her a breath. Each time I clamp my hand back over her face, I indicate the unfolded napkin with her hand. She doesn't give an inch. After five rounds of counting and gasping, the napkin still lies unfolded. Once Helen senses the pattern, she doesn't struggle at all. I decide to raise the stakes. The sixth time I count to forty-five. The seventh, fifty. Her resistance leaves me stymied; when the count stretches past forty, she fidgets a little but doesn't relent.

I linger at fifty for a few rounds, uneasy with going higher. "I'll hold my breath too," I decide, "and we'll see who the real daredevil is."

When we reach the upper forties, my lungs feel too large for my chest. At fifty-five my hands tremble, and I wonder if the air straining inside me will crack my ribs apart. At sixty my chest seems light enough to float away, my bulging eyes hot as boiled eggs. By sixty-five I'm pounding Helen's hand against her napkin, begging her to pick it up. At sixty-eight she surrenders, folding the napkin quicker than a skivvy on washing day.

I sink to my knees, sucking air into my dried-out throat, too shaken to appreciate my success. Before she can throw another fit, I take Helen by the hand and lead her to the door. She resists until she feels me turning the key. We go to the back door, and I let her out into the warm sunshine. She darts away over the lawn.

At the sound of the door Mrs. Keller approaches from one of the outbuildings. "Miss Annie, is everything all right?"

"It is."

"I was waiting in the little house so . . . so I wouldn't hear." She looks aside, a halo of pink creeping from her hairline. "Did Helen eat from her own plate?"

"She did. With a spoon. And she folded her napkin."

A broad smile lights up her face, the first smile I've seen untinged by shame or melancholy. "Oh, Miss Annie," she breathes, taking my hands in hers, "Miss Annie." She presses the back of one of her hands to her mouth to hold in her tears as she looks at me. Her eyes glow blue as the sea.

Pride swells like another heartbeat within me, so large it threatens to leak from my eyes. I could stand like this forever, in the light of those shining blue eyes.

"How did you ever manage it?" she wonders, shaking her head.

I think of Helen's small feet kicking at nothing as I held the napkin over her face, and my pride shrivels into a black lump. My hand finds its way to my forehead. Dizzy, I shake my head. "I can't. I . . ."

"You poor thing," Mrs. Keller laughs, hugging me

to her side, "you're exhausted." She leads me like a child into the house and up the stairs. At my door she says, "You rest now. I'll look after Helen so she doesn't bother you." Closing the door, she pauses, turning those glowing eyes upon me once more.

I hold myself in place until the door clicks shut behind her. Relief melts me from the inside out. I throw myself onto the bed and let the tears come.

Chapter 15

*I very soon made up my mind that I could do nothing
with Helen in the midst of the family.*

—Anne Sullivan to Sophia Hopkins, March 1887

All my work is for nothing. Within a single day what
little Helen's learned unravels more quickly than a
frayed stocking. What with all the starts and stops and
doubling back, trying to teach Helen anything is as infuriating as reading with Tilly Delaney in the almshouse.

Crazy little Tilly may have been prone to fits and
wild with thoughts of escape, but she knew her letters,
and if I promised to help her run away from time to
time, she'd read to me. Trouble was she'd turn half a
dozen pages at a time and never remembered from one
day to the next where we'd left off—unless a jailbreak
figured into the story. Sometimes Tilly's voice would
halt, her body would stiffen, and she'd squeak and
gasp. The first time I put my ear down close to hear
what she was trying to say, I felt foam at her lips and
was terrified. But I soon learned to sit and wait until

the fit passed, and by and by she'd sit up, wipe her mouth, and go on with the reading—but like Helen, she never began where we'd stopped.

When we sit down to the next meal, Helen eats from her own plate only long enough to make a fool of me. As soon as the family applauds my accomplishment, she resumes her wandering. She's wily enough to take refuge from my fury in the captain's lap. Even my temper isn't strong enough to make me rip the child from her doting father's arms.

If I try to brush Helen's hair, she yelps, and Mrs. Keller swoops in to save her. When I refuse her a sweet, she screams, and the captain demands peace. If I correct her table manners, the entire family cringes. When she runs from my lessons, Mrs. Keller shields her.

Each time she kicks up a fuss, her parents rush to her side, though I've yet to see Helen cry from anything but anger or frustration. It doesn't matter how reasonable my demands are, or how unreasonable Helen's desires—tears are a crime. I think the captain in particular would let her run wild, naked, and filthy, feasting on nothing but cake and jam if it would keep her from crying.

And what about me? I have no shelter from Helen's abuse, no encouragement, cheer, or any sign at all that the Kellers understand my struggles. My heart is pitted with their indifference. Only a crumb of praise would be nourishment enough.

Oh, they're polite to me, of course. Hospitable,

even kind. But after so many days with no progress, I feel more and more like an extended houseguest, another of many small inconveniences life with Helen forces them to bear.

When Helen cries, though, I become an ogre in their eyes. I can't help it—it's useless for me to try to teach her language or anything else until she learns to obey me. Every lesson is an endurance trial, though all it takes to subdue her is a bit of backbone. But how can I discipline her under the family's nose? This place is stifling me, and Helen, too, though she doesn't know it. If only I could help her realize, as I did, how much more she could be.

*   *   *

From the moment I hear tell of places where the blind are taught to read and write, my mind is set. "I'm going to school when I grow up," I proclaim. Some of the inmates laugh at my grand notions, scoffing at the idea that a blind child could learn anything at all. "She'll be walking out of here someday on the arm of the emperor of Penzance," they jeer. Even Jimmie says, "You ain't either. You're going to stay here with me." But when their backs are turned, others tell me, "Sanborn, Frank B. Sanborn is the man you want to see about going to school." Time passes, and my conviction never wavers. I nurse my dream in secret, imagining a day when I can read for myself, without begging Tilly to lend me her eyes.

When Jimmie dies, the hope of school is all I have left for comfort, but no one cares. One solemn old woman scolds, "Education doesn't make any difference if the Lord wills otherwise."

"I don't see what the Lord has to do with it," I flare back at her. "And all the same, I'm going to school when I grow up!" After that they mutter at my insolence but leave me be.

* * *

How I wish the Kellers would do the same. No matter where I go, I never fit. Too wild, too willful, even for my own family. At Tewksbury my eyes made me a nuisance, and my notions were too grand. At Perkins, too, I was all wrong. Poor and ignorant, a Catholic among Protestants, I could have told them things about the world outside their fine homes that would have stripped the giggles from their throats. And what am I here? The contrary, outspoken northerner.

Next morning I'm only brushing Helen's hair, but she bawls like a bloodhound on the trail. When Mrs. Keller bursts into the room, she finds me sitting on the edge of the bed with Helen in front of me. My knees clutch Helen's sides, keeping her arms at bay, and my booted feet are crossed round her middle. I'm wielding the brush with considerable force, one hand grasping Helen's throat and chin to stop her jerking about.

"Miss Annie," she begins, clasping her hands, "is this really necessary?"

"It's this or shave her head," I rumble, tightening my grip on Helen.

"But Miss Annie—"

"You do it, then," I cry, thrusting the brush at her. I turn Helen loose, and as she blunders toward the feel of her mother's footsteps, I see a shiver of terror pass over Mrs. Keller's face. She takes a step back and Helen crashes into her.

"I can't control her, Miss Annie," she cries. "You know that."

The look on her face siphons away all my fury. Fine lines lie etched all along the edges of her delicate mouth, and her eyes swim with hurt. I slink from the bed, pulling the Perkins doll with me, and put it into Helen's thrashing arms. The tide of her anger turns, and Helen retreats to the corner with her plaything. "Oh, Mrs. Keller," I sigh. "Don't you see? The problem isn't Helen, it's you."

"Me?" She looks stung.

"All of you. You and the captain and Miss Eveline. You've given Helen nothing but pity, and it's turned her into a tyrant."

"We've been through this more than once," she says, shaking her head. "How can I expect her to behave any other way?"

"You expect better behavior from the captain's

hounds than from your own daughter. She needs discipline, not coddling."

"How can I discipline her? She doesn't understand."

"She understands plenty—even a dog understands when his master scolds him, and Helen's smarter than any dog I know. She knows all she has to do is throw a fit or dampen her cheeks, and the world is hers. She understands what you don't—that when you or the captain are here, I have no power over her."

"What would you have us do? We're her parents."

At last I can speak the words that have been brewing in my head: "Let me take her away somewhere."

Her head jerks up. "Away? Why?"

I understand her fear. The idea frightens me a little.

"I've tried everything I know. I can't win her love—she won't have any caressing from me. I can't win her confidence because she accepts everything I do for her as a matter of course. There's no coaxing or compromising with her. She will or she won't, and that's the end of it. Sympathy, affection, and fairness mean nothing to her. I've studied, planned, and prepared, but nothing I've learned fits. All I know is that I can't accomplish anything in this house. As long as Helen can run to you for protection, she won't learn a thing."

"Does she need protection, Miss Annie?"

The word strikes me like a barb. "What do *you* think, Mrs. Keller?" I blurt, displaying all my wounds at once: a broken tooth, bruised and battered shins, arms decorated with scratches and bite marks. "And if you ever scrub those filthy hands of hers, you'll find most of my skin under her nails!" Mrs. Keller's eyes flutter across my injuries. She reaches for me, then draws back to rub at a sore spot above her own elbow.

"I won't say I'm not harsh with Helen," I tell her, my tone softer, "but you've never found a mark on her, have you, now?"

She shakes her head, then asks, after a moment, "How long would you keep her?"

"Until she learns to obey and depend on me. A few weeks at least."

For a long time she says nothing. I feel my hand moving in and out of the silence like a needle through cloth. I look down. *P-l-e-a-s-e,* I'm spelling to myself. *Please, Mrs. Keller, please.*

She doesn't speak for so long my knees begin to ache, but the quiet hangs too heavy to disturb.

Finally she looks up and says, "I'll talk it over with the captain."

The captain. Oh, all is lost now.

I nod at Mrs. Keller, my head reeling. She goes out of the room. My feet carry me to my trunk and I open it. Back and forth across the room I wander, packing. One way or the other I'm sure to be leaving this house. Wherever I'm going, I may as well be ready.

The trunk fills quickly, but there's one thing more. I go to Helen's corner and scoop up one of her old dolls from the pile. Dropping it into her arms, I snatch the Perkins doll away and escape to the rocking chair by the window.

There I curl round myself like a wounded animal and rock. Hugging the doll to my chest, I close my eyes and wait for the fear and frustration to drain out of me.

Chapter 16

We had a terrific tussle, I can tell you.

—ANNE SULLIVAN TO SOPHIA HOPKINS, MARCH 1887

"Miss Sullivan," Captain Keller booms, "you and Helen will move into the little house next door just as soon as we can get it ready." I don't know which of us is more relieved. He seems almost giddy.

He's thought of most everything already: "We'll rearrange the furniture, air the place out to change the scent of it, then bring Helen there after a long ride so she won't know where she is. You'll have to share the old bedstead, but you'll have all the comforts." I even agree to let her parents look in on her every day, so long as Helen doesn't realize they're there.

So now I sit in my own little bower, waiting for Helen to arrive. They've been gone for almost an hour already. I can't help pacing the large front room. Everything is ready. All our clothes are put away, and Helen's toys are waiting for her. The fire is built up so the place feels cozy. I even have my own servant, young Percy, to tend the fireplace and bring our meals from the kitchen.

I haven't felt this hopeful since the day my sight was restored, breaking the world open like an egg before me. There were still ridges and bumps under my eyelids, but it didn't matter one whit. I could see the Charles River, the windows in the school buildings along its shore, even count the very bricks in their walls. When I threaded a needle without using my tongue, I nearly melted with joy. Best of all, I could make out words on a page. Dizzy with independence, I snatched up every bit of writing I could find—books in print and raised type, discarded newspapers and magazines—and devoured them all, from the crime columns to Shakespeare. During dull classes I sat in the back and squinted at the books and papers in my lap for headlines about the Tewksbury investigations, turning the pages so quietly my blind teachers and classmates couldn't hear them rustle. On days when my eyes throbbed and the tiny letters swam before me, I saved the scraps of newsprint until I could beg someone to read them for me between classes.

At last I hear the *clop-clopping* of horses' hooves on the lane. I run out onto the little piazza, parting the honeysuckle vines to watch them approach. As always, Helen refuses to be led, so her parents herd her up onto the porch and inside. She reaches out as she goes, looking for something to lay her hands on, and her nose waggles like a rat's as she searches for her bearings.

Mrs. Keller walks her to the seat of the bay window and unfastens Helen's coat and bonnet. For a moment Helen sits quietly, feeling the seat and window ledge. Mrs. Keller waits, watching, her hands pressed together before her mouth as though she's praying.

While Helen absently fingers her surroundings, Captain Keller takes his wife gently by the shoulders and tries to guide her away. Mrs. Keller is reluctant. She cranes her neck to look back at Helen, and her feet move slowly, as if she's coaxing them with each step. Anxiousness creases the captain's face—he looks as if he's trying to escape a deathbed scene.

"Go," I tell them as Helen begins groping the air where she expects to find her mother. I'll never be able to tear them apart if Helen gets her hands on them.

Finding no one, Helen's eyes widen and she grunts, slapping at the empty air with both hands. I nod at the captain. "Please, go now!" Captain Keller spins his wife about and propels her out the door. I slam it behind them and lean my back against it.

Frantic now, Helen stumbles and lurches toward me. Her terror is contagious. I cross myself and brace against the door. When she touches me, it takes her only an instant to recognize me. Horror-struck, she scrambles away. In the middle of the room she stands quite still, rubbing her cheek—the gesture for her mother. When no one comes, she rubs harder and harder, her face turning red to the roots of her hair. Finally she throws back her head and howls.

I don't dare touch her. She screams until she quivers, the sound so ragged I wonder if it won't tear her lungs apart. When her breath fails her, she slumps to the floor, lashing and squalling like an alley cat.

"Whisht, now. Whisht," I whisper, my lips trembling. The soft sound brings no comfort. I only remember my father, how he'd try to hush my screams first with the whiskey-dampened word, then with his fists.

Eventually Helen kicks and screams herself into a sort of stupor. She lies on the floor, her breath sharp but regular, her eyes glazed and blanker than usual.

She's alone, and she knows it.

The sight of her like this makes my chest constrict. I know how it feels to be alone, yet I took Helen's fear for granted. Now it shames me. I ache to gather her into my arms and press kisses into her hair, to tell her that nothing here will harm her. But I know I can't comfort her. Nothing can. If I try to touch her, she'll only lash out at me, just as I did when the nurses tried to wrench me from Jimmie's deathbed. I kicked and scratched and bit them until they dropped me on the floor and left me, a heap of pain beyond words.

Beyond words. The description is so apt for Helen, I'd laugh at the thought if I could squeeze a breath past the ache in my chest.

We're so alike, Helen and I. If I could only reach her,

her whole life would change. And perhaps mine, too. What would it be like, I wonder, to have someone love me again? I look at her, abandoned on the floor like a pile of rags. How could she love me after all I've done to her? I'm not even done with her yet. I suppose I'll have many more battles with the little woman before she learns the two essential things I must teach her: obedience and love. And then, perhaps, language.

When supper comes, she stirs at the scent. We don't have a table, so I leave Helen's plate on the floor beside her. Abandonment is no match for her appetite—she eats heartily with her fingers. I don't protest as long as she stays out of my plate.

After supper she seems brighter and devotes herself to her dolls. It's an amusing and pathetic scene. I don't think she has any special tenderness for them—the rough way she handles her cloth-and-china brood makes me wince. My fingers itch to scoop them up one by one and shelter them from Helen's mechanical rocking, dressing, and feeding. But if I go near her, she coils her muscles and swings a fist at me. Instead I perch on the edge of the window seat and feast on the sultry evening air as the round moon rises.

At last Helen yawns and digs at her eyes with her fists. Leaving my roost, I dangle her nightgown over her like a morsel on a string. To my surprise, she takes the bait and undresses quietly, then crawls into bed. I stand over her, marveling, as she burrows into the quilts.

Her curls glow like honey and molasses in the moonlight. The look of her makes me recall the sympathetic way the priest, Father Barbara, would rub my own hair when he made his rounds through the almshouse. I wonder how Helen's curls would feel between my fingers. I kneel beside the bed, scarcely daring to breathe. My hand floats over her head, stroking the thin layer of air that tingles with life above her.

"Ah, you're my girl now, aren't you?" I whisper.

My girl. A smile warms my face; I like the sound of it. Humming to myself, I rise and tidy the room, stacking our supper dishes and arranging Helen's dolls in a row along the bay window. I offer a word of comfort to each of them as I smooth their dresses and straighten their limbs, keeping my voice low so Percy won't hear as he tends the fire. Well satisfied with our quarters, I undress and slip under the covers beside Helen's warm little body.

When she feels me next to her, she leaps from the bed like a spark from a fire. "Now what?" I wonder, raising my head from the pillow. I scoot over to Helen's side of the bed and pull her back in. Arms flailing, she rolls herself right back out onto the floor. Hanging my head over the side of the bed, I reach down and lay a tentative finger across her hunched shoulder. Like a rankled crab, she waves a threatening arm my way, then scuttles across the floor.

"Lord above," I groan, climbing out of the bed. The chill of the floorboards against my bare feet makes me shiver. Wrapping a shawl round myself, I march to the window and grab a doll at random—a big, pink-cheeked, fuzzy-haired member of the family—then wave it under Helen's nose.

"Here, sleep with her instead." Backing toward the bed, I try to lure Helen under the covers. She follows only as far as her arms will reach. Exasperated, I fling the doll to the floor at Helen's feet and sulk.

Next I try cake. Helen follows the scent to the edge of the bed, but when I lay the mouthful on the quilt just out of her reach, she grunts and slouches to the floor in a pout.

I know if I were willing to lie on the floor, she'd sleep in the bed without me. I'm almost tired enough to do it. My eyes ache from squinting through the firelight; they're dry and rigid as two panes of glass every time I blink. I'd love nothing more than to curl up under a blanket and close them for good. But now that I've wrested Helen from her indulgent parents, I'd be a fool to let her cow me, too.

With a sigh I resign myself to the storm I'm about to cause, then bend over and toss Helen into the bed. The sight of her face as she bounces across the mattress chokes a laugh out of me. Her furious jabbering puts me in mind of a chipmunk's chatter.

My amusement doesn't last. When I try to climb onto my side of the bed, Helen crawls away. I race round the foot of the bed and block her. She howls and moves aside. From one end of the bed to the other the battle rages. At every turn Helen finds me barring her path. Each time she touches me, she screams with fear and frustration, until I'm ready to scream myself.

"Stop it," I cry at her, shaking the bedstead with both hands. "You're the monster here, not me!"

I lunge across the mattress at her, crazy with the fury, but she dives under the bed, out of my reach. Blind to reason, I drop to the floor and plunge in after her. The advantage of size keeps Helen just out of my grasp, but I wriggle along behind her, taking up the chase as we emerge on the other side of the room.

The rampage roars on for another hour at least—round and round the bed, over it and under it too. I've never seen such strength and endurance in a child. More than once Helen climbs the wooden headboard to avoid my acid touch. I even have to strip her, shrieking, from the heights of the bedposts.

Nothing I do holds her. I can't keep a grip on her limbs or pin her down with my own weight. Thrashing, bucking, kicking, or biting, Helen finds a way to squirm away from me every time. She has an uncanny knack for seeking out my tenderest spots for abuse—clamping her teeth onto the soles of my feet, slamming her palms against my nose, jabbing at the soft flesh under my ribs, or sinking her sharp little heels into my breasts.

Finally exhaustion and rage drive me outside myself, and I tear the quilt from the bed, obeying an impulse I hardly understand. Perched on a pillow near the headboard, Helen seems wary of the shuddering bed as I yank the covers from the frame.

Panting, I creep toward her, clutching the quilt to my chest and dragging my feet softly across the floor so she won't sense my footsteps. With a wild whoop I unfurl the quilt like a canopy over Helen's head, chortling as she tries to bat it away. Working quickly to avoid her sailing fists, I bring the corners of the cloth together at her ankles. A sharp tug topples Helen from her feet, capturing her like a rabbit in a snare. She claws and howls from inside the makeshift sack, but I pay no attention. Instead I roll her up tighter than a caterpillar in a cocoon, allowing her only the luxury of air. All she can do is yell, but that doesn't keep me from straddling the whole bundle to keep her from unrolling herself.

As the minutes stretch by, her screams melt into a sort of drone, and I struggle to hold my eyes open. They're so sore I feel as if my eyelids are dragging over a layer of sandpaper each time they droop.

By the time Helen bays herself to sleep, the fire's died down to nothing but a glow. At last I roll over and close my eyes. A wave of heat pours over them, until I'm sure they've turned to liquid. The last thing I'm aware of before I drift away is Helen inching herself away from me, even as she sleeps.

Chapter 17

*The more I think, the more certain I am that
obedience is the gateway through which knowledge,
yes, and love, too, enter the mind of a child.*

—Anne Sullivan to Sophia Hopkins, March 1887

Our first fights are brutal but short lived.

The entire first day Helen will have nothing to do
with me and plays with her dolls more than usual.
Over and over again she wanders to the door, touches
her cheek, and shakes her head. Seeing her so docile
and homesick makes me sick at heart, but I show her
no mercy. I insist that she dress, wash, and eat like a
civilized human.

All that long day Helen persists in contesting every
point to the bitter end. The battles are no easier here,
but at least without the Kellers looming over my shoulders, I can discipline her without feeling like a sneak
thief.

Every moment she tries my composure in one way
or another. It's as if she senses my struggle to control

myself. Before long I begin to believe she's trying to bait me into mistreating her.

But I don't give in.

My muscles shimmer with unspent anger when she deals a blow I can't repay, for fear of mirroring my father's senseless floggings. When she hurls herself to the floor in a tantrum, it takes all my strength to anchor myself against the window seat until she's spilled every drop of her energy. Hardest of all is keeping her sealed inside this place when I can plainly see she's thirsting for a familiar touch. But forlorn as she seems, Helen still spurns the slightest brush against my skin, flaring my compassion into pain. Each time she cringes from me, I press my fists to my mouth to keep from striking her. By the time the urge passes, I can feel the print of my teeth against the insides of my lips.

In bed at night I cry—angry tears—but they bring no relief. I only grow angrier. Beneath it all, my sympathy for Helen makes me rage against myself. The last thing she needs is pity.

In my despair I curse myself for slighting the Kellers' small kindnesses. I imagine them in the big house, playing card games while Captain Keller tells droll tales of hunting expeditions gone awry or men who dared to eat watermelons the size of which would sicken a giant.

Of them all, the one I'm most like in the world is Helen. I could almost laugh to think of it. She's every bit as wild and willful as I was. No one but Jimmie has ever been able to tame me, and he did it without ever lifting a finger. I remember his voice, drifting across the space between our cots, *You're going to stay here with me, forever and ever.* But in the end he was the one who left. If I could convince her to love me, Helen could never leave me. She doesn't know it, but Helen needs me more than Jimmie ever did. She knows nothing about me—none of the things that matter to everyone else, at least—and still I'm not good enough for her.

The irony of my plight bites at me as I sink to sleep: Helen lies only inches away from me, and I've never felt so alone in my life.

Our grappling continues the next day, with less zeal. As the day wears on, Helen's resistance falls away piecemeal. Perhaps she senses that with no one to rescue her, it's much less trouble to submit to my will than challenge my fists. By evening I think she fights only because it's all she knows how to do.

That night I watch her eating her supper with a spoon and try to feel triumphant. The thought of ceasing our violent rows leaves me giddy, but something troubles me. I can't take my eyes from her.

"Something isn't right," I murmur, but I can't see what it is. For long minutes I watch her spoon go up and down, up and down, with methodical precision. I feel sick, and I don't know why. Then it hits me.

The way she moves is wrong.

Eating is one of Helen's true delights, but tonight she takes no pleasure from it. She's listless, as if the food has no taste. For days I've fought for calm, and now it frightens me. It's as though a light's gone out.

By midmorning my anxiety curdles into irritation. Helen's next trick is almost effortless but every bit as infuriating: She sits still as a lump of clay, doing nothing at all.

At first I'm paralyzed with the thought that I might have snuffed her spirit out. But when I try to force her to wash and dress herself, I sense a spark of something in her. I don't know how, but I know she's paying attention. Something in her lies coiled up tight, waiting for a reaction. If she were an affectionate child, I'd call it mischief. Knowing Helen, I'm inclined to name it spite.

"And what am I to do, then?" I wonder aloud. I'm not about to play nursemaid to an oversize rag doll. It's an ingenious tactic she's come up with; I can't very well punish her for not resisting. "But if I ignore you, you still manage to get your own way, now, don't you?"

Just then Percy arrives with the breakfast tray. He's hardly through the door when Helen's nose twitches—barely a quiver—but I have my answer. "Still in there, are you? I thought as much."

I bring the tray and Helen's clothes over to her. "I'll give you one more chance," I tell her, handing Helen her dress and pinafore. She lets them fall to the floor like so many leaves.

A sharp sigh escapes me. "Fine." Kneeling beside her, I take Helen by the arm and yank her down next to me. With her hands in mine, I touch her fingers to the pile of clothing, then to herself, then to my nodding head. "Get dressed."

She does nothing.

"Well, listen to this, then." I drag the breakfast tray over and push her hands from item to item: *clothes, Helen, breakfast, nod.* Then the gestures I'm sure she'll understand: *clothes, floor, breakfast, no.* When I shake my head, a tremor of dismay flickers across Helen's face. "That's right, my girl, get dressed or starve."

With a dramatic flounce she slumps to the floor, throwing herself across the heap of clothing like a beached fish. "Grand, just grand," I mutter.

For a quarter of an hour I watch Helen lie there, limp as a worm, while my breakfast cools. "Not giving up any time soon, are you?" I growl, scooping up the tray and stalking to the bay window. With the tray balanced atop my crossed legs, I glower at her over my plate. When I open the window to let the breeze waft the scent of the food through the room, she doesn't budge.

By the time Captain Keller passes by the window

on his way to the office, I've heard Helen's stomach gurgle more than once.

Striding up to the casement, he calls, "Good morning, Miss Sull–Sullivan." The sight of his daughter sprawled across the floor startles him into choking on my name, but he manages to keep his composure. Until he sees Helen's untouched breakfast sitting next to my empty plate, that is. Then his eyes narrow and his brows hunch together.

"Miss Sullivan, do you have any idea what time it is?" His tone is deliberately even.

"I don't," I tell him, returning his glare level for level.

My insolence stuns him for the length of a breath. "Miss Sullivan," he says again, a dash of venom lurking under his tight-lipped gentility, "it is nearly ten o'clock. Don't you think Helen has been deprived of enough in her life?"

Anger radiates through me until I hear it pounding in waves against my ears. I have it in mind to let him know that she hasn't been deprived of nearly enough. But the edge in the captain's voice warns me I'm walking a fine line with him.

"I'll deprive her only as long as she disobeys," I return, battling to keep my voice level. "She'll have her breakfast as soon as she dresses herself." He doesn't answer. I risk a jab. "Is that so unreasonable, Captain Keller?"

His jaw stiffens. "When Helen is ready, send Percy

to the kitchen for a plate of hot food," he directs, lifting his chin to glance coolly down at me.

"Hot food is a privilege," I snap. "If Helen wants a warm plate, she'll have to dress sooner."

Puffing himself up with authority, the captain tugs at his cuffs, then straightens his collar. "Miss Sullivan," he begins.

I feel myself shrivel.

"Do you know what we said to the Yankees when Lee surrendered to Grant?" he asks.

My head jerks up. "I don't."

"'You only won because you had more Irish,'" the captain finishes, and marches away toward town.

Openmouthed, I watch him go. "I won," I murmur to myself.

And it only took ten days.

Maysville Jr.-Sr.
High Library

Chapter 18

The little house is a genuine bit of paradise.

—Anne Sullivan to Sophia Hopkins, March 1887

Helen holds out until just after noon.

Percy comes in with the dinner tray and stands in the doorway, befuddled by Helen, lying still on the floor amid her dress and stockings. "Walk right by her," I tell him, "and put it on the windowsill." When the smell of the hot food passes over her, Helen gives a little snuffle. Percy glances at me, his eyebrows raised. I shake my head and beckon him to the window. The minutes tick past without so much as a tremble from her. And then the slightest puff of a sigh stirs the tangled hair across her forehead, and I see her fingers creep across the floorboards toward a stocking. If I'd blinked, I would have missed it.

I feel a shift inside me as a smile breaks my face. "Take that cold dish of breakfast away please, Percy. It looks like Helen is ready for dinner."

From then on things are different. As if by magic I have not had any trouble at all with Helen since. Captain Keller stops in morning and night, but he never interferes. Both of them have tested my limits and found Miss Spitfire does not budge.

The first time I take Helen outside for a frolic in the garden, she pushes my guiding hand away and stumbles off the porch on her own. "Go on, then, if you think you know the way," I tell her.

Exploring with her feet, she shuffles along, her hands searching the air. Keeping myself between Helen and the big house, I follow along as she muddles her way toward the boxwood hedges.

As soon as she touches them, her confusion vanishes. She blinks, and without warning, gestures fly from her fingers, one after another. "What's all this?" I wonder, bemused by her enthusiasm. Mingled between motions I can't decipher are a jumble of elaborate pantomimes: She tugs at her chin as if pulling on imaginary whiskers, makes motions of hoeing and digging, mimes doffing a cap, milking a cow, and pumping water. I hold my breath, waiting for her to bolt, for the big house stands perhaps twenty paces away.

"Surely you know where you are now," I say aloud. To my surprise, Helen makes no move toward her home. She only picks her way along the shrubbery, never letting go with both hands at once. Then I understand. The bushes don't reach to the house, and there is no path here. With nothing and no one to guide her, the space between the buildings might as well be miles.

Now when we go out, I put my signs into her hands. Every afternoon we tour Ivy Green from end to end. Before long I've learned the name of every man and beast on the property and relayed them all into Helen's palm.

Her mind tantalizes me with glimpses of brightness. Already she can spell "doll," "cake," "card," "hat," and "key." She hasn't any idea what the signs mean; I could have trained her just as easily to clap hands or turn in a circle instead of spelling. But it isn't important for Helen to make sense of what she's doing yet. What matters is her fingers don't hesitate to make the letters when I give her the objects. Laura Bridgman learned the same way—first matching the words to the objects by rote, then the great leap: understanding.

My only worry is Dr. Howe never mentioned *how* he got Laura to make that leap. I don't think he knew himself how it happened. All I can think to do is to do my best and leave the rest to whatever power manages what we cannot.

Even beset with such difficulties, I'm thankful every minute for this little bower. We eat our meals out on the piazza, shaded by vines so luxuriant they cover the garden beyond. Percy brings the meals and takes care of the fire, so I can give my entire attention to Helen.

The more I find to busy her restless limbs, the more normal she becomes. When I first came, her movements were so insistent that no one could help feeling there was something unnatural and almost weird about her. The simplest things, stringing beads or crocheting, consume enough of her attention to funnel some of that frenzied energy away. Now when the boredom creeps up on her, she comes to me, filling an imaginary string with beads or working her fingers under my nose like the crochet needles until I put something in her hands. I have little fear of her fists now, though she still refuses to be led and knocks everything in her path aside rather than step askance. Far be it from me to judge her for that, though—she blunders into far less with her hands and feet than I do with my tongue and temper.

In the open fields I show her how to tumble, turn somersaults, and roll down hills. We bend our backs inside out, arching over the ground like bridges. Sometimes I enlist the servant children for a game of crack-the-whip, and Helen frolics among them like any child her age. When they tire and try to drift away, she stands before them and snaps her arms back and forth to show she still wants to play.

In the late afternoon we return, panting and scented with tramped grass, sweat, and sunshine. From time to time I smuggle crickets home in my pockets, then drop them into Helen's hands for the impish delight of seeing her splutter with astonishment as they spring from her palms like living firecrackers.

When the weather turns temperamental, we stay indoors and exercise with a set of dumbbells until she's mastered the movements I learned to the tune of Verdi's "Anvil Chorus" at Perkins. Captain Keller is so tickled by his daughter the strongman he's promised to fit up a gymnasium for her. One cloudy afternoon she feels the rumble of thunder even before I've heard it and goes searching for the weights herself, pumping her arms up and down until I understand and pull the dumbbells from their shelf.

On especially good days I take our lunch out into the yard, and we picnic under the trees. Helen gathers wildflowers to weave into clumsy chains, and I pluck blossoms from the azalea bushes to fit over our finger-tips like caps for elves. Bedecked as finely as any fairy queen, she snuggles into a large grandfather oak with a crotch of roots like an armchair. While Helen sits, stroking a sheltered clump of violets, I play the muse, spelling songs and poems into her free hand.

I only wish I knew more music than laments and tavern songs. Once, a palsied old man told me he knew a reel called "Annie Is My Darling," but nothing so rare as a fiddle existed in the almshouse, and no tune of any kind would sputter from his toothless gums.

Even the melodic poetry my father used to recite for me in Gaelic is no more than a hazy recollection. Little wonder–I couldn't understand a word, but the mournful sound of it thrilled me. Giving up on the words, I hum with Helen's hand on my throat, trying to recapture the cadence and coax the contours of the sounds from my memory.

In the end I recite everything from nursery rhymes to Byron and Shakespeare. Helen pays most attention to the childish ditties and finger plays, for I make my hands leap and skip like rabbits to their bouncy rhythms. The pertinence of "Bessie's Song to Her Doll" tickles me so, I recite it over and over.

> Matilda Jane, you never look
> At any toy or picture-book.
> I show you pretty things in vain–
> You must be blind, Matilda Jane!
>
> I ask you riddles, tell you tales,
> But *all* our conversation fails.
> You *never* answer me again–
> I fear you're dumb, Matilda Jane!
>
> Matilda darling, when I call,
> You never seem to hear at all.
> I shout with all my might and main–
> But you're *so* deaf, Matilda Jane!

Matilda Jane, you needn't mind,
For, though you're deaf and dumb and blind,
There's *some one* loves you, it is plain—
And that is *me*, Matilda Jane!

I inch toward affection with her, but Helen dances out of my reach. She accepts my touch, so long as I'm spelling, helping her dress and wash, or teaching her a new pattern with the beads or crochet needle. If I try to kiss her or hold her in my lap, she wrests herself away. At least she's stopped screaming at the touch of my skin.

At night I dare to caress her. Propped on my elbow beside her, I trace the fine bend of her brow or brush my fingers under the curve of her chin. Such a pretty child she is, with her brown-gold hair and round cheeks. I wish I could draw her in close to me, to feel the murmur of my voice humming the old Irish songs.

Instead I have to settle for the Perkins doll. She nestles near and tight, rests her cheek against my skin, and lets my eager fingers stroke her curls. But oh, how I wish she had breath and weight and warmth.

I try to remember I've been hired as Helen's teacher, not her friend, not her companion. I came to earn a living, and kisses from a blind child, no matter how dear, won't pay my way in the world.

"And yet, touch is all she has," I whisper to the doll. "Why isn't mine good enough?" I'll confess, those first days I was hard on her, but I never harmed her. I never thrashed her without reason, the way my father beat me.

And what if I had? Children forgive so much for the sake of a tender moment. I know I did.

Many a night my mother hid me at the sound of Dad's footsteps, yet there were times when I'd crawl like an adoring pup into his lap. I remember how often he came stumbling home, the bawdy songs spilling from his lips. Verses from "John Barleycorn" and "Ugly Mrs. Fen" made my poor mother stir in her bed, but she never said a word unless he started into "Easy and Slow." Then she'd be up shouting, "Shut that mouth in front of your daughter!" Sometimes I'd dare to creep from my corner, for if he spied me, he'd wink and whisper the last verse for my ears alone:

> Now if ever you go to the town of Dungannon,
> You can search till your eyes are empty or blind.
> Be you lying or walking or sitting or running,
> A girl like Annie you never will find.

Oh, how I loved him then.

If I can find a reason to love as worthless a man as Thomas Sullivan, I don't know why Helen can't feel the kindness in me.

Chapter 19

*You will be glad to hear that my experiment
is working out finely.*

—Anne Sullivan to Sophia Hopkins, March 1887

How strange to think there was a time when my fingers
and lips worked separately. It's been only a few years
since I learned to spell my own name, and now all day
long I spell-speak, the curve of Helen's fingers riding
the waves of my hand like a small boat. When Captain
Keller appears at the window, I have to wind my
fingers together to keep them from weaving words as
we talk.

Today Helen and I have a long conversation about
"mug" and "milk."

No matter what I do, Helen confuses the two. Each
time she points to the mug, she spells "milk." When
she spells "mug," she mimes pouring and drinking.

"That's what I get for trying to show two words
at once," I sigh. I should have given her the empty
mug first and added the milk later. Now everything's

muddled. I wonder if she thinks the milk is part of the mug.

"Milk," I tell her, dipping one hand into it and spelling into the other. I pat her hand, and she makes the letters *m-i-l-k*. Next I let her drink the milk and make her spell it again.

"Now it's empty, you see?" She feels the mug inside and out. "Only a mug. No milk." I spell *m-u-g* over and over into her free hand. "Let it settle, now."

One at a time I give her a doll, a hat, a key, a card. She makes all the word-shapes without a single mistake, and I pop a nibble of cake into her mouth after each one. Then I turn the tables: I spell the words, and Helen picks out the matching object. Again no mistakes. Until we come to "mug." She touches everything on the table but seems confounded. Finally she brings her hands to her lips as if she's drinking a cup of air.

"Ah, no," I groan. As an experiment, I spell *m-i-l-k*. "What do you think of that?" She points to the mug. "That's what I thought." I try to smooth the frustration from my forehead with my fingertips. The sockets of my eyes sting from the effort of watching her nimble fingers leap from one letter to the next.

Helen reaches for my hands, looking for her customary bit of cake. I shake my head. A scant few days ago this would have erupted into a tussle. Now a shake of my head vexes Helen but doesn't provoke her fists. To be safe, I busy her hands with a crochet needle and a length of red Scotch wool. She learned a simple chain stitch earlier this week and seems intent on making a chain to reach across the room.

While she works, I pace, pondering the mug-milk difficulty. It seems as if she's confused them both with the notion of drinking, but I don't dare introduce another word into the mess. How can I unsnarl the words in her mind when she doesn't know what a word is? All this time I've been preaching that my arbitrary signs are superior to Helen's gestures—now I'm kicking up a fuss over confusing two words that don't mean a thing to her one way or another.

I hear Helen scuffling about and turn to see her crawling across the floor, yarn in hand. She's tied one end of her chain to a chair leg by the window. She crochets incessantly, scooting toward the opposite wall as she stitches. Bored with my thoughts of mugs and milk, I watch Helen labor over her yarn. I'm anxious to do something else—exercise, romp in the garden, anything—but she doesn't slow.

"Will you never stop?" I flop on the bed, grumbling, "Inventions of the devil, sewing and crocheting. I'd rather break stones on the king's highway than hem a handkerchief." Serves me right, I suppose. It took me nearly two years to finish sewing an apron at Perkins. Finally the teacher shut me into a closet with the model skeleton as punishment. I only laughed and rattled its expensive bones until she came running to let me out again.

When Helen succeeds in stretching her woolen snake from the chair to the fireplace on the other side, she plunks herself down on the hearth and pats her arm.

I join her on the floor and pat her head. She doesn't flinch. Ignoring me, she lifts the length of wool to her cheek and rubs it lovingly against her skin. Her affection for the first work of her hands puts a twinge in my heart. Quickly, I lean in and peck her cheek. She jerks her neck away and turns her attention to the wool. That's all. No screams, no fits. Still, it's enough to make a shiver of resentment run through me. I smother it, making my hand spell *w-o-o-l*. After I pat her hand, she duplicates the word. "Like a little spelling machine, you are. Drop in a coin, turn the crank, and out comes a word."

And what good is all this spelling? Sometimes I think Helen will learn quickly enough, by and by, that everything has a name. Other times I feel lost. I don't know what I'm doing, really. I'm only feeling my way myself, every bit as blind as Helen. How do I move forward? How do I connect one thing with another? I wish I knew this work was taking root somewhere in Helen's mind. All these words, do they linger in her fingers after her lessons are through?

A few days later I have my answer. On his nightly turn by the little house Captain Keller announces, "Miss

Sullivan, I've brought an old friend to call on Helen."

My heart sinks. Helen and I spent half the afternoon struggling over "mug" and "milk" with no success. I don't have the strength for another battle. Hands clasped, I go to the window, trying to keep the pleading tone from my voice. "Captain Keller, we agreed. No visits."

He chuckles and holds up a hand, nodding. "I know, I know. But I assure you, Miss Belle won't undermine your authority." The captain slips two fingers into his mouth and whistles a shrill note. A large, red-coated setter trots round the corner and positions herself at his feet with military precision. "Miss Sullivan, meet Belle. One of the finest hunting dogs in the county, in her day. And the most patient creature this side of Mobile, where Helen is concerned."

Belle rolls her great eyes up at me and blinks. Her tongue sags from her mouth.

"Now, you don't mind seeing if Helen recognizes her old playmate, do you?"

I turn to Helen, bathing one of her dolls in our washbowl. I worked her hard today–too hard, perhaps, judging by the way she jostles the doll. She deserves a treat. "No. No, I don't mind a bit, Captain. Bring her round front."

I let Belle through the door. From across the room she gives a contemptuous sniff in Helen's direction, then skulks to the window, making no attempt to attract her attention. I imagine she's been roughly handled by her little mistress more than once.

To our surprise, Helen takes no notice of Belle's arrival. Usually the softest step makes her throw her arms out, searching for anyone within reach. Captain Keller shrugs.

After half a minute Helen's nose comes to life. She dumps the doll in the basin and feels round the room, sniffing as she goes. Near the window she stumbles upon the dog and throws her arms round Belle's neck.

At the sight of her clinging to the dog I notice Captain Keller's smile quaver. Masking a sniff, he lifts his chin and clasps his hands behind his back. I feel a jealous sting myself and swipe my knuckles against the corners of my eyes.

Her fit of affection done, Helen plops down next to Belle and takes one of the dog's paws in her hand. "What's she doing there?" the captain asks, watching Helen manipulate Belle's claws with her fingers. Puzzled, we lean as close as we dare. Helen's face wrinkles with concentration as she works to shape the dog's claws under her hands. Belle only blinks and yawns.

After a minute she gives up and balances Belle's paw on top of her fingers. I gnaw my lips, biting back a grin as I watch Helen's fingers move.

"D-o-l-l," I translate for the captain. "She's teaching the dog to spell!"

Chapter 20

*Yesterday I had the little negro boy come in when
Helen was having her lesson, and
learn the letters, too.*

—ANNE SULLIVAN TO SOPHIA HOPKINS, MARCH 1887

The next day, Friday, I invite Percy to attend Helen's lesson. I'm eager to see what she'll make of a pupil with hands and fingers instead of paws and claws. Besides, showing Helen that other people can make these signs might spark some understanding of their usefulness.

Percy's spent time with Helen before, that much is clear. At first he teeters on the edge of his seat. Each time her hands move, I notice the corners of his eyes squinch up; he's too proud to flinch but shrewd enough to brace himself.

Percy has trouble from the beginning. Helen demands to follow every bit of his lesson, blocking his view of his fingers and mine with her meddlesome hands. Percy's task becomes as awkward as carrying on a conversation with an ill-mannered hound prodding its nose into all the wrong places. Helen leaves him no choice but to learn the letters with his fingers instead of his eyes.

Despite her blindness, Helen proves a much quicker pupil; poor Percy isn't used to recognizing shapes with his hands. Even easy signs like *d*, *c*, *o*, and *l* give him trouble, which puzzles me. The signs look as similar to the written letters as four fingers and a thumb can.

"Percy, you can't read, can you?"

He looks at me as if I've no more sense than a goat. "Read," he scoffs, rolling his eyes like Viny. "'Course I can't read."

Grand. I've insulted him and made a fool of myself. There's no more chance for a black boy in Alabama to learn to spell than I had in the poorhouse. If God had seen fit to give me a brain as quick as my tongue, I'd have the brightest mind in creation. Hoping the speed of my tongue will redeem itself, I keep talking.

"This is reading hands instead of paper. When you learn the letters, you'll have your own secret language."

"Yeah," he says, fixing his dark eyes on me. "How?"

"I learned the letters in Boston. No one in Alabama will understand you unless we teach them. You'll be able to spell under anyone's nose, and they'll be none the wiser."

He nods, trying not to grin at the thought of such mischief. Earnest now, he trudges through the lesson.

For better or worse, Helen's attention never falters. Keeping a close grip on both our hands, Helen mimics my every move for Percy, right down to prompting his response with a pat of her hand. Eventually Percy gives up on his eyes altogether, shutting them tight as he memorizes the shape of a new word or staring off at nothing in particular when he works to recall the letters on his own.

Percy's mistakes delight Helen, and for once her pleasure isn't selfish. His struggles drive Helen to excel him, while at the same time she refuses to continue until he's mastered each new word. I've never seen her so ambitious. Somewhere in her head I sense a flicker of life—could it be something I've put there? My stomach flutters at the thought.

As the afternoon passes, Percy's wariness trickles away. Before long the three of us sit clustered in a ring, hands meshed like voices in song. I spell a word to Helen, and it passes like a melody from hand to hand. I show Helen; Helen shows Percy.

For the first time I feel like a teacher.

Helen proves a capable little schoolmarm too. She may be oblivious to the meaning of words, but she won't permit the slightest blunder in their spelling. When Percy confuses the letters, she makes him form them over and over again until she's satisfied. Then she pats his head with such vigor that Percy blinks and ducks his head like a goose with every touch. His smile flashes so brightly beneath Helen's hand that I begin to wonder if some of his slips are intentional. I'd like to hug him for it, but all I do is grin.

I relish Helen's eagerness, the way her hand lingers under mine, impatient for the next word. Buoyed by her enthusiasm, I give her hand a congratulatory squeeze each time Percy learns a new sign. She makes no objections, and my heart quickens.

When we've marched through all the objects Helen knows, I unveil the finale—two sticks of candy, courtesy of Captain Keller's morning visit. Percy licks his lips at the sight of them. "Is that store-bought?" he asks.

"It is. One for each of you, after you learn to spell it."

He eyes Helen. "Give Helen her stick before mine," he says.

I laugh and pat his cheek. His shoulder hunches up toward my hand, and his skin turns rosy as varnished cherrywood. "You watch closely," I tell him. "This once I'm giving you a head start." I spell "candy" for him, pausing between each letter. "Now, be ready when your turn comes. The sooner Helen gets her stick, the better." Solemn faced, he nods.

I turn to Helen. Never letting go of my end of the candy, I lay one stick across her hand. Her body shivers as she recognizes the treat. Smacking her chops, she scoots toward me. I half expect her to knock me aside and tear the sweet from my fist. Instead she huddles up close to me, tracing the candy's path to my pocket.

As I spell, Helen's muscles tense with concentration. At five letters, this is the longest name I've tried to teach her. I hope she has patience enough to learn it, and for Percy to learn it too.

I needn't worry. After a pat to signal her turn, Helen's fingers flit out the letters quickly as the beat of insect wings. She reaches for my face to feel my confirming nod. Instinctively I nudge my cheek against the heel of her palm. Her touch doesn't linger. She buzzes about, searching for her promised treat.

Beckoning to Percy with one hand, I stuff the candy deeper into my pocket with the other. "Do as I've done, Percy. Pat her hand. Ask her for the word."

Hesitant, he obeys. His request breaks Helen's attention from her search. "Keep your hand on hers, Percy, don't let go." I hold my breath, waiting for her reaction.

Slowly she turns to him. Holding the hand with Percy's perched upon it very still, she gropes with the other. When their free hands meet, she grabs his and arranges all ten of his fingers over her fist. Her face set firm, one hand still clasped on Percy's wrist, Helen moves her fingers from one letter to the next: *c-a-n-d-y*. Twice more she spells it, her movements precise as a drumbeat.

"C-a-n-d-y, c-a-n-d-y," I chant to him as Helen's fingers shift from shape to shape.

Satisfied with her part of the lesson, Helen shakes loose of Percy's grip, then cups her fingers over his.

My view blocked, I lean in and weave my fingers among theirs. Percy screws his eyes shut and folds his lips between his teeth. Determination hones their features into concentrated points as he begins to spell.

"*C* . . . *a* . . . same as 'cake,'" I whisper to him, scarcely daring to breathe. "Now the *n*." He pauses, fishing for the new letter. "Almost like *m*," I remind him. "Good. *D* like 'doll.' And now the *y*."

He freezes. I feel Helen fidgeting, her patience twitching away. She pats Percy's hand, prompting him for the rest of the word. His arm jerks at her touch. She taps again, more insistent, more like a smack.

It's no use. He's forgotten. Helen raps at his knuckles, demanding one more letter. His panic vibrates through the tightness of his locked fist. I could show him, tell him, before Helen dissolves into one of her furies, but the thought of cheating after so much success disgusts me. I make the sign behind my back, thinking how to hint at its shape. "Start with *i*, Percy, then add to it."

His pinky rises under my hand, then his thumb. "*Y*," he says.

Helen lets out a triumphant cry, frightening both of us breathless. My eyes fly open, surprising me, for I didn't realize I'd shut them. Helen flings her arms round Percy's head, practically mauling him with the force of her pride. My laugh rings through the little house at the sight of him squinting up between the clutch of her arms.

In the next instant he is forgotten. Helen's fingers patter over my frame, probing for her promised treat. I reach into my pocket and present a glistening stick to each of them—plain for Helen, stripes for Percy. His eyes feast upon the decoration. Before he can so much as lick it, Helen grabs him by the arm, hauling him out the door. Outside she plops down onto the edge of the piazza, yanking Percy to the floor beside her. There they sit, swinging their legs, sucking their candy like old chums. Propping myself against one of the posts, I ease myself to the floor beside them, hugging my knees to my chest.

Percy looks up at me. "Don't you have one?" he asks, waving his treat in the air.

I smile. "No, this afternoon's been sweet enough."

Chapter 21

My heart is singing for joy this morning.
—ANNE SULLIVAN TO SOPHIA HOPKINS, MARCH 1887

The morning starts like any other. Helen washes and dresses herself as I've taught her, but it falls to me to brush her hair. The brush is something she tolerates only because it's a point I refuse to compromise.

The change begins with a ribbon, a length of yellow satin from one of Mrs. Keller's forgotten sewing baskets. I've always loved pretty things, fine clothing especially. The weave of well-made cloth, the precision of neat rows of stitches, and the intricacies of lace and ribbons delight my fingers.

"Once upon a time," I muse as I guide the brush through Helen's hair, "there was a little girl named Johanna, but everyone called her Annie. Her father worked the Taylor farm, and Annie wished more than anything in the world to have a hat as beautiful as the Taylor girl's. Well, one day her father bought her a hat—a white one, with a blue ribbon and a pink rose." My hand stills a moment, remembering. The Taylor girl never had such a beautiful hat. Nor has anyone since.

Through brushing, I send Helen to the dresser to fetch the bit of string I use to tie her hair away from her face. Today, though, I've replaced the worn cord with the satin ribbon. Helen's wardrobe is plain and practical—no wonder, given her rough-and-tumble ways—but after yesterday's lesson she deserves a bit of finery to charm her fingers. Confused, she sweeps her hands over the entire surface of the dresser top, then gives up and brings me the ribbon wadded in her fist.

"Like this," I tell her, pulling the crumpled ball from her grip. "Smooth it over." Guiding Helen's fingers to and fro, I show her how to appreciate its fine surface.

Almost immediately she responds to the silky texture—her movements become nearly dainty, fingertips skimming across the ribbon's length like water bugs skating along the surface of a pool. Playful now, I take the ribbon up by its ends and shimmy it back and forth over the tip of Helen's nose as if I'm polishing the toe of a shoe. She wrinkles up her face in ticklish pleasure. I move to her chin, and she nuzzles against my swishing movements.

Hooking one finger round the ribbon, she tries to pull it from me. Her desire to touch it, her attraction to its softness, makes my heart thump. I snap the ribbon back and weave it between my fingers, then rub them across my cheek, like Helen's mother-gesture. When she senses my movement, Helen crowds in close to me. Finding my arm, she feels her way along to my shoulder, up my neck, and to my face. There she follows the movement of my beribboned hand. Her touch is abrupt and awkward, but it makes no difference to me. My breath comes faster at the feel of her fingers against my cheek.

Still not satisfied, Helen jerks my hand to her own face, dragging my satin-adorned knuckles from her ear to her chin. I will myself to stay calm, but the delight of it makes my skin ripple.

"I touched her," I marvel to the empty cottage. Who would believe it? I hardly believe it myself until I hear my own voice say it. My mind pauses, lingering on the moment. Unmoved as ever, Helen uses my distraction to unravel the ribbon from my hand.

Her fingers twisted in satin, Helen waggles her hand before my face. Daring now, I duck forward, brushing my lips across her fingertips. She squeals and jumps away, then capers forward, shaking the ribbon at my face like a banner. Heart racing, I snatch it from her, baiting her to come nearer. When she does, I capture her between my knees once more. She squirms at first, but I stay her with a touch.

"Here," I tell her, dangling the ribbon over her fist, "let's put it in your hair." I let her feel it, then move her hand to her hair. She muses a moment, then grabs the ribbon from me and presses it against her head.

"That's right, little woman." Feeling me nod, she pushes the ribbon into my hands and turns about, presenting her hair to me. Holding my breath, I draw her up onto my knee. Her body lurches once, searching for balance, then stills. I smother a gasp and gape at her.

Suddenly she sways again, motioning at her hair. I steady her with a hand at the small of her back. Impatient, she grabs a fistful of curls and shakes them at me. Fingers fumbling, I sweep a handful of hair into a bundle, then fasten it with a clumsy bow. With a tap I signal I'm through. Entranced by the decoration, Helen's fingers creep up into her hair, winding in and out of the ribbon's tails.

My steadying hand still rests at her waist, but she doesn't notice. I watch the way her fingers move, flipping the length of satin back and forth, back and forth, like a Jacob's ladder. Turned in profile, her misshapen eye is hidden from my view. I see only half of her face—the pretty half. I fancy it's also the bright half, the obedient half. Is this the side of Helen that let me touch her moments ago?

I scarcely dare to move, for fear of breaking the spell. The softness of the satin has almost bewitched her. I imagine the way it must feel, slipping between her fingers, warming like a second skin. Is there warmth and softness in Helen, too?

My arm laces closer round her, sounding for the depth of her tolerance. When she doesn't squirm, I take a chance. Quick as a hummingbird, I lean in and plant a kiss on Helen's cheek. Soft and sweet as an apricot.

She blinks. Her fingers cease twining through the ribbon, though she doesn't let go. Her free hand rises to her face, brushing as if she expects to feel something lingering there. Finding nothing, she reaches for my face, touches my lips.

I work my hand into hers. "Kiss," I whisper, forming the letters with unsteady fingers.

I feel as if a soft breeze has replaced the hot blood that so often thunders through my veins.

Puzzled, Helen reaches for my lips. I kiss her fingertips. Letting the ribbon loose, she touches my face with both hands. I spell "kiss" again, my voice too tight to speak the word. She copies the letters and mirrors my gratified nod.

My heart swells with a laugh while tears squeeze against my throat. The place where they meet feels ready to burst. I want to wrap my arms round her and rock her like a baby, but I quell the urge—the weight of my pent-up affection would smother her. Instead I press my cheek to hers for the length of a breath, then shoo her from my lap.

A shudder runs through me as Helen slides from my legs. The place where she sat feels blank. It's an ugly sensation. Desperate to shake it, I follow Helen across the room to where she busies her hands with the crochet needle. My lips brush her cheek once more.

She accepts my affection as a matter of course.

I want to throw the windows wide open and shout. I want to hug her again and again. But I can't–I have to keep from vexing her with my attention. I need to fill my arms and thoughts with something besides the memory of our momentary connection.

My hands dance with excitement as I draw out pen, ink, and paper. Joy spills across the page: "A miracle has happened! The light of understanding has shone upon my little pupil's mind, and behold, all things are changed!"

I gaze at Helen and smile dreamily at the thought of Mrs. Hopkins reading these pages to my friends. Helen looks so serene, laboring over her chain of wool with gentle hands. To think the little savage learned her first lesson in obedience, and finds the yoke easy! The great step–the step that counts–has been taken. I write grandly of my achievement to Mrs. Hopkins: "It now remains my pleasant task to direct and mould the beautiful intelligence that is beginning to stir in the child-soul."

I should know by now that with Helen nothing is so easy as it seems.

Chapter 22

When she is in a particularly gentle mood, she will sit in my lap for a minute or two.

—ANNE SULLIVAN TO SOPHIA HOPKINS, MARCH 1887

Helen will not return my caresses.

For a little while the days floated by. Morning, noon, and night I found reasons to pass near her, smoothing her hair or patting her cheek on my way, if only to remind myself of her approval. At night I drifted to sleep with my temple resting against her shoulder, or my fingers twined into her curls while the Perkins doll watched from her place among her china sisters on the window seat.

But as time passes, the magic of our brief connection fades. Helen allows me to touch her but makes no response. Before long the charm of such one-sided affection evaporates. I find myself holding back. She never cringes or swats at me, never grunts or pulls away. She gives me as much regard as the table edges and doorways she bumps into from time to time.

I hadn't expected there could be something more difficult to live with than the wild Helen, who screamed if even my skirts brushed near her. This phantom child is far worse. Each time Helen disregards my touch, I feel a strange patter in my stomach, as if I'm violating her somehow. Her indifference digs at me; I come away from her feeling splintered.

"'A devil,'" I mutter to her, borrowing the harsh words from Shakespeare, "'a born devil, on whose nature nurture can never stick; on whom my pains, humanely taken, all, all lost, quite lost' . . ."

By the third night I find myself stealing into the rocking chair with the Perkins doll. But even her oblivious submission doesn't satisfy me—her cold china skin only leeches the warmth from my body into hers. Weary, I set her aside and try to soften her abandonment with dulcet words.

So, we'll go no more a-roving
    So late into the night,
Though the heart be still as loving,
    And the moon be still as bright.

For the sword outwears its sheath,
    And the soul wears out the breast,
And the heart must pause to breathe,
    And Love itself have rest.

Though the night was made for loving,
    And the day returns too soon,
Yet we'll go no more a-roving
    By the light of the moon.

In the afternoon I let Helen outside for a good romp in the garden. With the ivy and flowers at her fingertips, Helen is at her happiest. Watching her fondle the mimosa and azalea blossoms or press her face into the wide leaves of the ivy should bring me some comfort. Instead I feel as if something in the center of me has sunk like a weight, closing my throat and pulling the corners of my mouth down with it. How can she be so tender with the plants and leave me to wilt?

I might be able to teach Helen what words are, but can I teach her to feel? The way she brushes off any sort of affection makes me wonder if she's capable of becoming anything more than a two-legged pup who can fetch and carry and sew. "At least a dog wags its tail at a gentle touch or a kind word," I sigh, feeling myself droop. Irritated with my own self-pity, I straighten up. "There's many a heartless human, but not a beast in history has uttered a single word," I tell myself. And Helen spoke at only six months old.

I glance over her head toward the house. No one in sight. I do wish Mrs. Keller would look in to see us the way the captain does. I miss her company. I'd like to hear thoughts and voices besides my own, and my eyes are too sore to be scouring books for comfort. But

Mrs. Keller quarantines herself from Helen absolutely. Perhaps complete separation from Helen is easier than tempting herself with secret glances from afar. Still, her affection won't be stifled—I often notice Mrs. Keller going to and from the kitchen, and she spends hours at a time tending her lavish flower beds. It's no coincidence Percy delivers meals more sumptuous than anything served in the big house or that sweet-smelling flower cuttings find their way onto Helen's tray.

I wish I could find such an easy path to Helen's heart.

By the time Captain Keller stops at the window that evening, I'm so glad to see another feeling human I could throw my arms round his neck. I settle for sitting as near the casement as I can manage. When he sees Helen stringing beads, he remarks, "How quiet she is!"

It's small praise, but I can't help beaming at his amazement.

The captain leans against the windowsill, one fist propped on his hip. "Helen seems a different child entirely, Miss Sullivan."

I answer carefully, so as not to betray my nagging dismay. "She is. I haven't seen a fit of temper in nearly a week. She's every bit as stubborn, but she doesn't resist my control. A shake or nod of my head has become a fact as apparent to her as the difference between pain and pleasure." Indeed, I've built such strong links between the two ideas, they've likely become much the same in Helen's mind. But I don't dare tell him that.

Nodding, he surveys the ordered space of the room. Reading the satisfaction in his face, I puff up my chest like a mother hen on her roost. Then his eyes fall on Helen's abandoned supper tray. Almost a third of her food lies untouched. His beard jerks as his lips straighten.

"How is Mrs. Keller, Captain?" I ask, hoping to distract him.

"Fine, fine," he answers with a wave of his hand. "Is that Helen's supper there?"

"It is."

"And why haven't you given her the rest of it?"

"I have. She doesn't want it."

"Doesn't want it?" He crosses his arms and drums his fingers against his elbows. "She must be homesick. If this keeps up, you'll have to return to Ivy Green."

My stomach twists like an overwrung shirt. "But she's so much more docile, Captain Keller," I implore. "If she doesn't spend half the day whirling about like a cyclone, she's sure to eat less."

"Perhaps, Miss Sullivan, perhaps," he says, rocking back and forth on the balls of his feet. "But the child must eat. See that she gets enough. I shall not see her deprived."

I nod. I don't agree with him, but for once I'm afraid to argue. Worn as I am by loneliness, the idea of returning to Ivy Green hardens my worries into a cold brick. I've worked so hard to bring Helen under my control. Even if the Kellers are willing to discipline her, I'm not fool enough to think Helen will obey another master without a fight.

Turning to go, the captain smiles and shakes his head. "She's learned more than I thought possible, Miss Sullivan." The words tumble from my ears to my stomach like a tubful of wet laundry.

More than he thought possible?

What have I taught Helen these last ten days? Nothing remarkable—how to wash herself, feed herself. How to knit a scrap of wool. I've taught her no more than the average imbecile can learn—keep clean, keep quiet. And this from a child who spoke at six months old. Would the Kellers settle for so little?

A fluttering catches my eye. I look down and find my own fingers spelling out my agitation. Clasping them together, I thrust my hands between my knees to steady them. But I can't keep my thoughts from whirling.

I don't know which is worse: returning to Ivy Green and the endless tug-of-war over Helen's behavior, or the idea that Helen's own parents would leave her mind to rot in her head so long as she keeps quiet and doesn't make a mess. It's hardly more than anyone expected of me, and I was nothing but a blind poorhouse orphan. It's hardly more than anyone expects of a well-trained pet.

The thought drives me from my seat by the window, propelling my feet round and round the place where Helen sits stringing her beads in endless patterns. "I'm supposed to be a teacher, not a monkey trainer," I tell her. The procession of beads continues: precise, perfunctory. "But I've hardly taught you a thing, have I? I've done no more than mold you into a copycat."

Picking up one of the strings, I run it through my fingers like a rosary, examining its design. This is not one of the simple wood-glass-wood combinations I showed her. The pattern is more than a dozen beads long.

"And no one but me is willing to delve into your head," I marvel. "They'd sooner starve your mind than see a few untouched morsels on your supper plate."

Unless I can prove Helen's mind needs as much nourishment as her body.

Chapter 23

*"M-u-g" and "m-i-l-k," have given her more
trouble than other words.*

—ANNE SULLIVAN TO SOPHIA HOPKINS, MARCH 1887

From that moment I throw myself wholeheartedly
into Helen's education. Following Dr. Howe's example,
I make myself hold regular lessons at set times. I line
the objects in a row and drill her again and again. But
I spend the whole day long spelling, pouring words
across her palm like streams of water.

All the day through I talk into Helen's hand. Not
only single words, but whole conversations. When I
speak, she touches my throat, feeling the buzz of my
voice. Nothing like thought crosses her face, but the
vibrations hold her transfixed, and I wonder if she has
any sort of a memory of her own voice.

Trouble is, I don't know how to gauge Helen's
progress. Measured in the amount of cake Helen
consumes each day—I give her a bite as a reward each
time she spells a word correctly—our work would fill a

pantry. But even that mountain of cake hasn't taught her a thing. She copies new words day after day, never forgetting the old ones, and never shows a hint of understanding. It's as if her fingers have a memory all their own, separate from whatever sense lies sealed behind her eyes and ears. If it weren't for the cake, she'd show little more interest in spelling than she does in the hairbrush or washbasin.

And yet she prompts me to spell words now, patting my hand as though she wants to know the name of something. But the way she moves is so mechanical, her face so flat and uncurious, that I'm sure she's only mimicking me. She's come to expect a finger motion to match any object we touch, the way rain follows thunder. When I spell a word at her request, she ignores it, using nothing but her gestures to get what she wants. And she never bothers to repeat a word unless I cue her with that same patting.

One day under the pecan tree she finds a broken robin's egg. She brings it to me and pats my hand. I spell "egg," then double my hands on the ground, the way I saw her do that first morning in the kitchen. She squats and cups her hands like a bowl with the egg inside.

N-e-s-t, I spell. She grunts and searches through the grass. "Looking to raid the nest, you little vixen?" Instead she finds a pecan and brings that to me. I spell "pecan," and her search shifts from eggs to nuts.

When her pockets are full of pecans, she makes a

hammering motion. I spell "hammer" to her, making her repeat it, then she makes her way along the path to the barn and kicks at the door until a stable hand comes running.

"Pat her hand," I command him. He gives me a sideways glance but does as he's told. I stand close by, praying for Helen to spell to him. Instead she shakes his fingers loose and makes the hammering motion again.

I slump with disappointment.

Shrugging, he plucks a wooden mallet from the wall of tools, and Helen scampers off.

As I watch her crack open the pecans on the brick path, I seethe with frustration. The feeling reminds me of my blind years—tantalized by the half sights around me, with no way to make sense of them.

Sitting in Uncle John's pasture, I'd twine my hands through the grass, twisting the long blades. My fingers told me they were slim and smooth as snakes' tongues, but my eyes couldn't distinguish one blade from another. No matter how near the ground I crouched, I saw only a blur of green as featureless as a woolen blanket. Knowing my eyes couldn't show me the grass as it truly was made me rip great clumps of it from the ground.

I grow to love and hate her homemade signs. She has signs for all sorts of things—people, objects, and even verbs. Many of them she's invented since we've come to the little house. They prove her instinct to communicate, but I'd like to scream each time she creates a gesture for a word I've already taught her, like "bead," "hammer," "crochet," "dumbbells," and "crack-the-whip."

Almost every day one of her signs confounds me. One afternoon she tugs at my sleeve in the middle of a lesson. Linking her fingers, she brings the heels of her hands together, like a hinge.

"What's this?" I ask. With a shake of my head I continue my spelling. Frowning, she shoves my hands aside and repeats her sign. I shrug. Her face constricts, and she works her hands in the jawlike motion once again, then waits.

I don't have the first notion what she wants. I haven't taught her the name of any object that opens and shuts that way. "What is it—a book? A door? Chattering teeth?" When I don't respond, she pushes her hands into my face, pounding them together. Surprised by her intensity, I bar her with an arm and try to sit her back down. Her eyebrows furrow; heat rises from her skin. Huffing, she gropes over the table. Nothing in reach satisfies her. Once more she levers her hands before my face, imploring me with her unnamed want.

I shake my head. I can't even tell her I don't understand, not really.

The anger grips her before my eyes. Her hands slow; her body shakes. I watch her chest heave faster and faster, see her fists ball. She makes the sign one last time, then throws back her head and wails.

"I don't know how they could take this as mindlessness," I whisper as the sound penetrates me. "Anyone can see your brain is screaming to be let loose. But you don't even know what you're struggling toward, do you?"

Even in Tewksbury I had it better than Helen—I knew there was a way out of my prison.

* * *

One day the wards rustle with quiet commotion. "Investigation," I hear them say. "A commission from Boston." Amid the whispers of public scandal and outrage I hear the name Sanborn, and my heart begins to race. It's been four years since I learned that name—*Frank B. Sanborn is the man you want to see about going to school,* someone said—and this is the first time I've heard it outside of my own dreams.

My situation is so ridiculous I want to sob with frustration. I'm not even certain Mr. Sanborn is among the commission, and blind as I am, how can I possibly recognize a man I've never met? But if I am to get out of this place, this is my only chance. From ward to ward I follow the tight bunch I hope are the investigators, straining to hear something that might tell me if any of them is Mr. Sanborn.

By the time they reach the big stone gate, I'm quivering with the desperation. Hurling myself into their midst, I cry, "Mr. Sanborn, Mr. Sanborn, I want to go to school!"

I collide with a mass of legs and elbows. Woolen coat sleeves smear the tears across my cheeks. A hand grasps my arm. "What is the matter with you?" a voice asks.

Suddenly spent, I can only stammer, "I–I can't see very well."

"How long have you been here?" asks another.

"I don't know."

The voices rumble together, but they say no more to me. Someone pushes the hair from my face, straightens my apron. A handkerchief drops into my hand, and before I've realized what's happened, the men are gone. I stand there hiccuping, wondering what's to become of me, if anything at all. As I drag my feet away from the gate, my fingers find a bit of embroidery on a corner of the handkerchief, and once again I have a hope to cling to. Spelled out in fine floss are the initials FBS.

*   *   *

I wish I knew how to tell Helen that my spelling is her way out. "The key is in your very grasp," I whisper. My fists clench, then go slack.

Her breath spent, Helen sinks to the floor, moaning. The mournful sound of it makes me want to curl away and hide. I soothe her the only way I know how: I swing the door open, then lift her to her feet and coax her out to the garden. There she creeps under a hedge and buries her face in the broad ivy leaves.

"There's at least some feeling alive in you," I sigh. The thought brings little consolation. Can she possibly realize what makes her so miserable?

She can't tell a soul how she feels. She can't even think it to herself. No wonder she spends her days kicking and screaming—what else is she to do with herself? Watching her huddle among the cool leaves for comfort, I wonder if she lashes out in fear as well. She must feel so small when the rage overpowers her. I shake my head at the thought of it: This brazen tyrant could actually be terrified by her own feelings.

Determined to spare her another frustration-tempest, I concoct a multitude of strategies for breaking into Helen's mind. I teach her verbs—"sit," "stand," and "walk"—guiding her from one action to the next like a puppet on a string. I try to connect my words with her gestures, spelling *m-o-t-h-e-r* if she rubs her cheek, *e-a-t* when she makes a chewing motion, or *b-a-b-y* when she rocks her arms back and forth. Nothing changes. In desperation I spell out the very ideas I'm trying to force into her head letter by letter: *A word is a symbol. It stands for an object. Its meaning is the same to everyone who uses it.*

Day after day the mug-milk difficulty torments me. No matter what I do, Helen persists in confounding the two. I fill glasses, teacups, and bowls with milk, hoping to distract her from the notion of the mug entirely. I let her follow my hands pouring the milk from one vessel to another. Each time she tastes the liquid, she answers my tap with *m-u-g*. When I produce the mug to correct her mistake, she switches her reply to *m-i-l-k*. I snatch it from her and fling the horrid thing into the garden. A moment later my resolve returns, and I march outside to retrieve it. Set on unsnarling Helen's confusion, I return to the little house and begin all over again.

One evening at milking time I take Helen to the barn. After setting the mug under a particularly patient cow, I hold one of Helen's hands under the streams while I spell "milk" into the other.

No good. *M-u-g,* she insists.

With a groan I flop my head onto the cow's warm flank.

The next day I leave the mug at the little house and wet Helen's lips with milk hot from the cow's teat. Even with the taste on her tongue, she spells "mug" when I ask. I squirt a creamy jet into her face, my throat gravelly with the discouragement.

I wonder if a better teacher could have unlocked Helen's thoughts by now. I have more faith in Helen's mind than I have in my abilities. At least I know there's something inside her, scrabbling to get out. What is there in me but worry and doubt? Dr. Howe called for patience and zeal in educating the deaf-blind. I don't know if I have either. Back on Uncle John's farm I had patience enough to lure birds into my bare hands, but I'm so flummoxed by Helen's stalled progress I'd like to shake her until the pieces of her lessons fall into place.

By the end of the week Captain Keller insists Helen return to Ivy Green. I can hardly argue. I asked to keep her sequestered only as long as it took for her to obey and depend upon me. I've accomplished that much, at least. But there's no guarantee my teachings will hold, and I have never been good at leaving anything behind, good or bad. So much has already slipped through my fingers.

*   *   *

When the visiting priest, Father Barbara, says he's taking me away from Tewksbury for an operation on my eyes, I cry and tell him I don't want to go. My sight is little more than bewildering swirls of colors, like ladies' skirts always dancing before me, but I don't care. In the months since Jimmie died, Tewksbury has become all the home I have.

I'm right to be afraid. When the doctors' work is done, I'm no sooner put to bed with a bandage over my eyes than another woman arrives, rescued from a fire. Her moans and screams tear through the ward, and the scent of charred flesh stings my nostrils. The talk I hear is of skin and cloth melted together, singed flesh sloughing off in pieces, and white bones shining through it all. A picture worse than anything I saw at Tewksbury forms in my mind, and I cry and flail until the bandage comes loose from my eyes and the nurses carry me away.

After all that, the operation isn't much use. All it does is turn the swirls into a blur. But away from the almshouse, I get a glimpse of another world. I help the sisters deliver baskets to the poor. From time to time I slip into Saint Patrick's Church to peer at the chalice and carvings on the altar. Often Father Barbara joins me there and chants the stations of the cross to me, or sits still and quiet in the pews, pretending to listen to a sermon. Other days we walk along the river Merrimac, hand in hand, and at night he reads to me of Saint Bridget, Saint Lucia, Saint Catherine. For a few days some friends of Father Barbara's take me in, a dark house where it's my job to wipe the dishes, and there I discover a piano. I bang away gleefully until someone yanks me from the bench.

When the next operation is done, there are no burn victims to torment me. The nurse is kind and lets me make lemonades, chipping ice from the great block in the kitchen myself and adding all the sugar I want. My eyes are no different, but every day calm-faced nurses fuss over me, and there are plates of fruit and slices of bread almost as soft and white as my sheets.

Before long the doctors decide they've done all they can with me. Father Barbara is gone, called away on duty. His friends don't want me back in their house, and the hospital can't keep me. Tewksbury looms before me. The thought of leaving this clean and decent place for what lies behind the stone gates of the almshouse makes the fear rear up like a cold wind inside me. Howling, I fasten myself to the doctor's leg until they peel me away.

*   *   *

The thought of the days ahead of me at Ivy Green, the dread of more clashes with the Kellers over Helen's discipline, makes that same cold fear whirl through me. We've taken one great step forward, and after this glimpse of success I have no intention of giving any ground back. But where will I find the strength to stand between Helen and the overindulgence of her parents?

Chapter 24

I have pointed out that the processes of teaching the child that everything cannot be as he wills it, are apt to be painful both to him and to his teacher.

—ANNE SULLIVAN TO SOPHIA HOPKINS, MARCH 1887

My heart pounds. My fingers, so used to moving when I speak, itch to spell. I clasp my hands in my lap and urge myself to be brave.

Across from me on the parlor sofa Mrs. Keller and Helen sit side by side, fitted together like the strands of a braid. Mrs. Keller strokes Helen's cheek with the backs of her fingers, softly as a kitten smoothing its whiskers. Behind them the captain stands with his hands resting one on each side of his wife and daughter. Seeing them framed in contentment, I wish I could join their intimate circle. I pray my words won't ruin the scene before me.

I draw a deep breath. "You must not interfere with me in any way."

The captain's face crimps like the mouth of a satchel drawing together. He glances down at his small family, then at me. His eyes tell me to be cautious, but they don't keep me from speaking.

"I know it hurts to see your child punished, and even more because of her afflictions. Whatever you think of me, I'll tell you, it's painful for me as well. But allowing Helen her way in everything is a terrible injustice." The conviction behind these words surprises me. The Kellers, too, look puzzled.

"An injustice," I insist, the words coming unbidden. "Not only to you and me, but to Helen. You let her behave like a common imbecile, tolerating those fits. She's a bright child, yet you allow her to make a fool of herself with every tantrum. She may not understand the reason behind good behavior, but she's smart enough to mimic it. At least let her have that small dignity."

Mrs. Keller looks up, her eyes bleary with tears. I can't guess the emotion behind them. "But she has so few pleasures, Miss Annie."

Exasperation makes my words harsher still. "That's no excuse for bad behavior. The world outside Ivy Green won't bend to her will, Mrs. Keller. And neither of us will be with her forever. Who in their right mind will cater to her whims when you're gone?"

"Miss Sullivan–," the captain begins. I know where this is headed. We've been down this road more than once.

I cut him off. "There's no reason to deprive her of anything–as long as she's civil to the rest of us. I'm willing to grant Helen any luxury you can bestow her, provided she earns it. Let me hold her to what I've taught her—be consistent—and she'll stay as calm and reasonable as she is this minute."

"Do you propose, Miss Sullivan," the captain says, straining for courtesy, "that we simply hand over our authority as parents?"

I gulp, willing myself to hold my chin high in the face of the captain's indignation. "Any interference will undermine everything I've accomplished these two weeks. Helen may be deaf, dumb, and blind, but she's no fool. If she finds an easier path, she'll take it and never look back. For now she's tame, but given the chance, she'd turn on you like a mad dog." I pause, chiding myself for the acrid words forming on my tongue. I smooth my face into dour seriousness. "I'd hate to have to take her away from you again." This is not entirely true, but it has the desired effect. Mrs. Keller looks stricken; her arms pull Helen nearer.

A lump comes into my throat. Why must I be so cruel? "Please, just let me have a free hand."

Mrs. Keller nods, wide eyed and fearful as a little child. I look to Captain Keller. Confronted with his wife's tears, he assents.

"You'll speak to the rest of the family as well," I prompt. He nods again.

A shiver runs through my body. It's done.

"Wouldn't you at least like to have a nurse for her?" Mrs. Keller offers.

I blink at the question, my emotion breaking into confusion. "A nurse? Whatever for?"

"To dress and feed and wash her. You'd have all your time to teach her."

"Helen's perfectly capable of all that. A nurse will only get in my way. Every simple thing we do is a lesson in itself. Besides, I don't need anyone else to look after."

And that is the end of that.

Only a few hours later my agreement with the Kellers wavers with the threat of mutiny. We sit round the supper table, before platters heaped with mounds of food sweetened and sauced with Helen's tastes in mind. In a sudden about-face Helen behaves long enough to earn me the barest morsel of respect before making a fool of me yet again.

She sits stock-still through the blessing, seemingly fused to her chair. Her hands don't wander from her own place. Her legs don't swing or fidget. The only movement at the table comes from the shifting glances of Helen's family, eyeing her as though they find her good manners distracting.

When Captain Keller takes his seat, I turn to Helen and put the napkin round her neck. As I reach for the nearest serving bowl, I hear a rustle next to me. The napkin has disappeared from Helen's neck. Her arm hangs limp at her side, fingers pointing to the floor.

Beneath her hand the napkin lies like a puddle on the ground. I steal a look round the table, hoping no one has noticed this breach of etiquette.

Captain and Mrs. Keller avert their eyes. Simpson uses the opportunity to steal the largest cut of meat from the platter. James sits with his chin cupped in his hand, one corner of his mouth turned up in a wry half grin.

Enjoying the show, James? I want to ask him.

For a moment I'm torn. I know Helen is pushing me. It's no coincidence this is the first trouble I've had with her in nearly two weeks. I can't afford to let her win even one small battle. But the way the Kellers refuse to look at me makes my stomach shiver. Can they truly bear to witness my discipline?

Only Miss Eveline meets my gaze. She gives a small nod, heartening as a wink. A surge of conviction runs through me. I can't back down now.

With as much grace as I can muster, I lean over and retrieve Helen's fallen napkin. Again I fasten it round her neck and turn to filling our plates as though nothing has happened.

Again I hear the napkin flounce to the floor. I pick it up and double-knot it beneath Helen's hair. Her impudent fingers scurry to the knot, working like rats gnawing a bone. When she succeeds in removing the knot—and a few strands of hair with it—Helen flings the cloth to the floor.

I'm up in an instant. Captain Keller draws a sharp

breath but says nothing. I yank the napkin back into place, winding the ends together so tightly Helen's skin wrinkles beneath them. In the time it takes her to unravel that knot I manage to stuff a few bites of food into my mouth. I'm the only one eating.

Triumphant at last, Helen whips the napkin into my face.

"That's it." This time I bind her neck against the chair with the napkin and clutch the ends in my fist. "She'll use a napkin whether she likes it or not," I announce. Resisting like an unbroken horse, Helen twists against the cloth until her neck glows pink with the rubbing. Everyone, even James, squirms in their seat. I have no pity for them; it's no worse than I felt when Helen reigned as mealtime tyrant. Mrs. Keller reaches out to comfort her daughter. I snap my head toward her. "You promised me a free hand, Mrs. Keller," I remind her. Defeated, she lays her hands deliberately flat on either side of her plate.

Within seconds Helen begins flailing at the table with her feet. The dishes leap like fleas with each blow. Stripping away the last shred of her dignity, she grunts like a laboring sow as she fights.

Fed up at last, I let loose of the napkin. Helen lunges for her plate. I shove it aside and jerk her from the table. In a flurry of temper we lurch toward the door.

"Miss Sullivan!" the captain's voice thunders from behind me. "No child of mine shall be deprived of food on any account."

Fury freezes me on the spot. I can't do anything but splutter, "Captain Keller, our agreement!"

"Agreement or no agreement, I am the child's father." His knuckles rap the tabletop with each word. "You shall not deprive her of food, Miss Sullivan."

Trembling with indignation, I push Helen from my arms. Tears spill down my cheeks. The words rush over my tongue like bile. "For the love of God, Captain Keller, have you no shame?"

Chapter 25

And they had agreed to everything.

—Anne Sullivan to Sophia Hopkins, March 1887

I don't wait for an answer. Storming from the room, I bang the door shut behind me. Only halfway down the hall despair overcomes me. Too exhausted to sob, I slump to the floor in the parlor doorway and cradle my head in my arms. From the dining room I hear roaring voices mixed with wailing. Someone, perhaps Captain Keller, bangs the table again and again, making the dishes clatter.

I have surely done myself in. They've tolerated my brazen temper before, but I've gone beyond the limits of propriety this time. If I could find the strength to climb the stairs, I'd pack my trunk and escort it to the train station myself.

None of the voices I hear belong to Helen. Fearful as they are, the sounds pouring under the door are too refined to have come from her throat. I imagine her making the rounds of the table, unaware of the clamor, helping herself to the neglected plates jittering on the tabletop. What has my outburst gained me, then? I've insulted my employer and given my pupil permission to act just as she pleases.

Will I never learn? It's Perkins all over again, with them rubbing my face in my shortcomings and me shouting back like some class of an idiot. "Laugh, you silly things," I cried once when they ridiculed my spelling. "That's all you can do to the queen's taste."

Fancying herself the queen, the teacher retorted, "Get out of this room and sit on the steps until the hour has passed!"

Blind with rage, I bumped into a desk, and the teacher snapped, "Go back and leave the room quietly." I kept on my way, and at the door I turned and shouted, "I will not sit on the stairs and I will not come to this class again!" I very nearly didn't. Mr. Anagnos threatened to turn me out if I didn't return to that class, and I wouldn't. Only the intervention of my other teachers saved me. But who will save me now? None of the shouting in the dining room is likely on my behalf.

In the midst of the commotion a small sound captures my attention. Different from the din in the next room, it makes me think of a bird warbling. Following the sound between lulls in the uproar, I find myself creeping into the parlor, half expecting to find a sparrow trapped inside.

My eyes on the ceiling, I lumber into the cradle and nearly send baby Mildred toppling. A cry erupts from her mouth, and I crouch to hush her before I cause any more trouble.

"Whisht, now, whisht."

Her face turns, brightening at the sound of my voice. It's been so long since I've felt a child's eyes upon me, I feel almost naked. Bashful, I inch my hand over the edge of the cradle. She grips my thumb with fingers sturdy as tulip stems. A hiccuping sob twists my throat. I've been so long with dolls and blind brutes I've forgotten how simple it is to reach another person.

Without letting go of her, I plop down on the floor beside the cradle. When I lean over her, Mildred stretches toward my face, burbling like a bluebird.

I am besotted, beguiled, and bewitched. Seeing her reach for me nearly cracks me in two. When I bend to scoop her into my arms, a tear drops from my face onto her fat cheek. She giggles. My own laugh nearly chokes me.

I gather her up close to my shoulder and feel her sweet milk-breath on my neck. As I walk her round the room, my hips sway gently as a waltz. The movement soothes me as much as Mildred. Soft as a dove in my arms, she nestles her head against my shoulder and sighs. Her smile, the touch of her dimpled hands, the way her eyes seek mine at the sound of my voice, all these simple things enthrall me. Mildred charms me so, I don't hear the dining-room door open, nor the footsteps in the hall.

"Was our Mildred bothering you, Miss Annie?"

The voice falls like a chip of ice between my shoulder blades. Heat rises to the tips of my ears. I wonder how long I might have been watched. My face tightens into a grimace. I wish I had at least had the sense to leave the child in the cradle if I was going to make a fool of myself.

Turning slowly round, I try to straighten up, to look less like a child fawning over a live baby doll and more like a proper governess. "I didn't mean–" I stop, seeing it's only Miss Eveline. Her smile is weary, but her kind eyes relax my grip on the baby. "The noise frightened her. I was only on my way upstairs to pack."

"Pack?" Eveline's smile drops from her face. She glances behind her, as if she, too, expects to be watched. Bustling silently forward, she nudges me to the sofa on the far side of the room. "You mustn't think of packing up now," she half whispers, placing a firm hand over my knee.

"But the captain–"

"Arthur is a pigheaded fool if he lets you go now, and I told him so."

My stomach clamps round this news. I have to will strength into my arms to keep Mildred from slipping to the floor. "You told him that? After I insulted him?" My eye sockets seem flooded with boiling water.

"I've told him before, you'll be Helen's salvation if he has the good sense to let the two of you alone."

"Salvation," I murmur, shaking my head. Eveline offers me a lace-edged hankie and goes on, rubbing my back like an infant's as I try to suck back the tears.

"I've always believed our Helen has more sense than all the Kellers, but there was never a way to reach her mind. Until you came. You're two of a kind, Miss Annie. If anyone can bring Helen back to us, it's you."

"Me?" My voice comes out a croak.

"No one here has strength enough to discipline her one whit." She gulps on a laugh. "Did you know she woke up one night at midnight, demanding her breakfast? And God love her, I gave it to her. I'm ashamed to tell you I fed her, dressed her, and began my day by moonlight." Her chin trembles. "I shouldn't have done it. I knew it then and I know it now, but I couldn't refuse her." She tries to catch her brimming tears with her knuckles. I offer the handkerchief. Her lips refuse to obey her impulse to smile. "You see, Miss Annie? Our love leaves us too weak."

Their love leaves them too weak? My chest collapses like a squeezed lemon at the thought. Is that what they think love is—unbridled indulgence? If that's all they can offer Helen, she's better off without them, as I was without my father. I've never known a weaker man than Thomas Sullivan, and what did his love do for me?

Once, he came to Tewksbury with a box of candy. I didn't know what to think when I saw him. How could he still exist in the world if Jimmie and I had to live in a place like that? And then he left, never to return. For Chicago, he said, where there was no end of work building canals and railroads. No one can tell me it was for love that our father abandoned us in that place, with nothing but a sorry little box of sweets for comfort. His only strength was in his fists, and that had nothing to do with affection.

Miss Eveline would have me believe I'm stronger than all the Kellers put together, but what if I want to love Helen too? Am I to believe there can't be strength and love together?

My chest heaves, and my heart turns over. Her family's lenience is no more use to Helen than that box of candy was to me. No matter what the Kellers and I think of each other, if I leave Helen now, I'm no better than my own father. The thought of her shut up in her own mind, like Jimmie and I were cast aside in Tewksbury, makes me tearful with shame.

"I . . . I'll stay," I whisper.

Miss Eveline sighs with relief and closes her eyes for a moment. "Now, you go upstairs and rest," she says, patting my knee. "Give Arthur and Kate some time with the child. You can start new tomorrow."

The mention of the captain sends a flash of fear through me. "But our agreement?"

"Arthur will keep his word." She squeezes my arm and grins. "It looks as though he does have some shame after all."

❖

I don't see Helen again until breakfast. When I arrive in the dining room, she's already in her place. Both the captain and Mrs. Keller say, "Good morning," with lowered eyes and here-and-gone smiles. James cuts his eyes at me, saying nothing. Simpson remains oblivious. Only Miss Eveline shows any ease at my presence.

As I take my seat, Helen pulls at my hand. A corner of her napkin is stuffed into the neck of her dress. Tugging my hand, she calls my attention to the new arrangement. I make no objection. She seems pleased and pats herself.

Breakfast begins with deliberate order, like a military parade. Soon, though, Helen's model behavior slows the meal like the final wobbling turns of a top. Conversations start and sputter out each time she demonstrates a new skill. Using a knife and fork together claims absolute silence.

By the end of the meal my cheeks glow apple-bright with smug satisfaction. Pressed tight together, my lips burn to trumpet, *I told you so!* but I manage to keep a handle on my dignity. As we leave the dining room, Helen takes my hand and pats it. My brow crinkles. There's no emotion to it, yet it's different somehow from the way she asks me to spell for her. Mechanically she pats me again. *Slap, slap.* No more to it than the sound of skin against skin.

And yet I wonder.

"Are you trying to make up?" I turn back to the table and pick up a napkin. If her memory carries this far, I wonder what effect a little belated discipline might have.

Upstairs I arrange the objects for Helen's lesson on the table as usual. The cake, however, I place high on the mantel shelf, out of the reach of Helen's hands and keen nose.

When she arrives, Helen notices the missing cake at once. Her hands grope the length of the table, then fly to her mouth. Like a fist, her face tightens into a concentrated bunch. Her consternation draws a snort of amusement from me.

"Try a taste of this instead, my little imp." Kneeling beside her, I pin the napkin round her neck, then tear it to the floor, shaking my head. She jerks with surprise, but I'm sure she understands my meaning perfectly well. Still, I repeat the performance several times to make my point.

To my surprise, she slaps her own hand two or three times and imitates my shaking head. A corner of my mouth coils into a smile. "About time you disciplined yourself." Satisfied, I nod, and we return to our lesson as usual.

But Helen's mind refuses to let go so soon. After spelling half the words, she stops suddenly. Her unaccustomed stillness halts me as well. As I watch, her brow constricts. For the first time it dawns on me.

"You sly little thing. Your body stops when your brain stirs, doesn't it?"

While I ponder this, Helen's fingers dance across the tabletop, searching. They close over the napkin like a cat's pounce, making me jump. Pinning it round her neck, she brings a hand to her mouth, then waits, expectant.

Hands on hips, I cock my head and consider her. "Is this an apology, then?" She gestures once more, smacking her lips, too. I slap the heel of my hand between my eyes. "It's the cake you're after, isn't it?" I spell the word, then tap her hand, and she mirrors it back, frantic with excitement. "I suppose this is a proposition—you'll be a good girl for a bite of cake." Her ingenuity pleases me, but frustration tinges the moment as well. As I retrieve the plate of cake from the mantel, my mind wrestles a simple question:

If her fingers know the word so well, why doesn't her brain grasp the way to use it?

Chapter 26

We visit the horses and mules in their stalls and hunt for eggs and feed the turkeys.

—ANNE SULLIVAN TO SOPHIA HOPKINS, APRIL 1887

After an uneventful breakfast on Thursday we go outside and watch the men at work. Much as I dreaded returning to Ivy Green, it's good to be part of a household again. Being near people buoys my spirits. Though I keep Helen nearer to me than anyone else, it's a relief to roam freely among the family, instead of sequestering ourselves in the little house.

"Morning, Miss Annie," one of the stable hands greets us, doffing his cap. I think he's Percy's uncle. "And how is Missy Helen today?"

"Very well, thank you," I say with a nod, and proceed to the cattle stalls. Helen particularly enjoys currying the horses, but the cows show far more patience with her probing hands. Obstructing Helen's path with subtle movements, I guide her to Ella, the gentlest of the herd.

Helen's clever hands miss nothing. She runs her palms over the entire length of the beast, alternately smoothing and ruffling Ella's hide. Before long the ruminating motion of the animal's jaw piques her interest. Cupping her hands under Ella's chin, Helen follows the rhythmic movement. Soon Helen's jaw rotates in imitation of Ella's, her lips jutting out like fleshy handles. I shake my head and grin.

When she tires of mimicking the cow, Helen explores Ella's head from her chin to the tips of her ears. With a sweep of her arm she takes in the shape of the cow's head, then stops still.

My eyebrow rises. "Are the wheels in that brain turning again?" I ask her.

With a grunt she thumps on Ella's skull, then her own. Impatient with my conversational spelling, she wriggles free of my fingers and pats the back of my hand. The motion is jerky and artificial, as though she's a puppet who can never appear completely real, no matter how skillful the puppeteer.

It's arresting, though, the way she's adopted that movement. She looks for all the world as though she's asking, *What's this called?* Each time I can't help hoping, but the way Helen disregards the words once they've reached her palm makes me sure they mean nothing to her. Her pat is little more than a grunt, to show her desire to have my hands move in their accustomed fashion. I treat her as though she's asking the question, only in hopes that if a day comes when her brain is truly ready to ask, her fingers will know how to do it.

This time I don't know what to tell her; I've spelled "cow" often enough, and there's nothing new within reach. My hesitation seems to convey my confusion. Groping for me, Helen pats my head, then raps on my fingers. I understand at once.

"H-e-a-d."

The word seems to evaporate the moment it touches her hand. When I prod her fingers, she spells the word back to me, her face dulled by the task. A lesson springs to life in my mind. None of it is likely to make sense to her—I simply want to give her the chance to notice the new word when it occurs as part of a larger sentence. I move Helen's hand back to Ella. *This is the cow's head,* I spell. Next comes her own body: *This is the girl's head.*

Her interest holds for half a minute, then she returns to the cow. I wince as her palm lands over Ella's eye. The gentle beast only blinks. Helen flinches at the swish of Ella's long lashes, as if a fly has tickled her. Gingerly she reaches back, one finger extended. The brush of the cow's lashes draws a garbled sort of chuckle from Helen's chest. She rubs the pads of her fingers along the tips of Ella's eyelashes, then tries her luck with her own eyes. Wooden faced, she swats at my hand again. This time I know exactly what's cued her.

"E-y-e." Helen spells it back at my request, and I continue the lesson. *This is the cow's eye. This is the girl's eye.* Indeed, the oversize orb of her left eye looks much like the cow's.

Oblivious to my lecture, Helen continues exploring Ella's face and body, picking out more resemblances. She bends Ella's neck from side to side as she twists her own neck. Plunking herself on the floor, Helen probes her kneecaps, comparing them with Ella's. All the while she requests no more spelling.

Until she reaches Ella's hooves.

Flummoxed, Helen runs her hands back up the length of the cow's legs, noting the ankle, knee, and shoulder joints. Up and down her own arm she goes, flexing her shoulder, elbow, and wrist. Then each of her finger joints receives a thorough kneading. Returning to the cow, Helen raps her knuckles against Ella's hoof. After a moment's stillness she touches my hand, indicates her wriggling fingers, then slaps at me to spell.

F-i-n-g-e-r-s, I reply. *Girls have fingers. Cows have hooves.*

She sits for another minute, working her fingers like a multitude of hinges. Suddenly she scoots through the straw to Ella's hind legs. After a brief inspection she pulls me to her side. With a jab she indicates the tip of her boot, waves her fingers as if they're dancing over piano keys, then jabs at her boot again.

It's my turn to be puzzled. "Boot fingers?" I ask with a shrug. In reply Helen splays her hand over the toe of her boot and bobbles her fingers again. A grin tickles my cheeks. "Toes," I laugh, bouncing the letters into her palm. Taking her by the hand, I guide Helen away before I have to explain udders.

We do a great many things all morning long—string beads, knit and crochet, do gymnastics. When noon comes, we go upstairs for an hour to learn new words. It's a dull practice, digging up what she's learned to see if it's taken root. Both Helen and I would rather be outside, with real things and experiences. Besides, it's much easier to teach her things at odd moments than at set times. But no matter how tedious these classroom drills are, they worked for Laura Bridgman, and I don't dare abandon them.

Before surrendering her to dinnertime, I remind Helen of the words we learned in the barn this morning. Quick as ever, she repeats the words as I identify her head, eyes, fingers, and toes. Curious about her powers of association, I strip off my shoe and present her with my stocking foot and a questioning hand. Without hesitation she confirms my faith in her mind.

T-o-e-s.

I don't know why pride blossoms in my chest. It's not as if her intelligence has anything to do with me. Still, I squeeze her clever fingers in mine, wishing she could sense how pleased I am. "You've a mind as bright and broad as the sky."

Silence. Her blank eyes gape at nothing.

I sigh and drop her hand. "If only you could touch it."

In the afternoon Mrs. Keller treats us to a drive into town to see Helen's cousin Leila and her family. The carriage churns tufts of dust from the roads, pecking my eyes with sandy grains. By the time we reach Leila's doorstep, I'm blinking through a layer of dusty sludge, and I'm sure my eyelids have puffed up like mushroom caps.

With a daintily gloved hand Mrs. Keller raps at the door. Once again her impeccable dress and manners leave me awed. Someday I wish someone would regard me the way I admire her. Anchored to Helen, I must look like a rheumy-eyed stray tagging along at her heels.

The door swings open, and Leila greets Mrs. Keller with a wide smile and a ringing voice. "Cousin Kate, come in!" She squats before Helen, presenting her hand for inspection. "And look at you, Helen, in such a pretty hat. I bet you're hungry, aren't you, dear?" she says as Helen sniffs at her like a bloodhound. Opening her arms to me, too, Leila says, "You must be Miss Annie. How nice to meet you at last. Cousin Arthur's told me all about you."

I nod, trying not to blanch at the thought of what the captain might have said. She pays my ghastly eyes no mind and pulls me across the threshold. Clinging to Leila's skirts, Helen's baby cousin toddles behind on unsteady legs as her mother whisks us into the parlor. The child grins up at me, and I'm suddenly glad I've come.

Despite the bother of my stinging eyes, I realize an odd sense of relief at seeing new walls and faces. Resourceful as she is hospitable, Leila gives Helen a bowl full of half-shelled pecans to occupy both her hands and her appetite. With Helen so effectively entertained, I feel suddenly free. Muscles I hadn't consciously tightened relax as Mrs. Keller and Miss Leila chat.

In between their conversation the women sprinkle dollops of affection and praise over Leila's little girl. She is perhaps fifteen months old and already understands a great deal. Eager to show her off, Leila tells the baby, "Go to Auntie Kate. Now give her a kiss." Awkward yet responsive as a marionette, the child obeys. It's perfectly evident that she recognizes a great many words—like "nose," "mouth," "eye," "chin," "cheek," and "ear," which she points out prettily when we ask.

"Give the biscuit to Miss Annie," Mrs. Keller says, patting the child's round baby behind. Waving a soggy biscuit, she wobbles toward me like a plump, bright-eyed little pigeon. I hold my arms out wide, and she stumbles into them.

"Does she talk yet?" I ask, taking her onto my lap.

Leila nods, her curls bobbing with pride. "'Mama,' 'Papa,' 'Nana.' And she calls herself Baby."

"Bee-bee!" the child echoes, smashing the biscuit between her fat hands.

"But she can't say 'eye' or 'ear,' or 'biscuit'?"

"No, not yet," Leila answers. "She babbles for hours on end, so it won't be long. Will it, Baby?"

"Bee-bee!"

Laughing, I hug her to me. "Kiss?" I ask. She lunges at me like a lecher, mashing her lips against my cheek. Warmth ripples down to my toes.

Woozy with pleasure, I slide her from my lap and send her toddling to her mother before my gratitude bends her delicate bones.

Chapter 27

You must see that she is very bright, but you have no idea how cunning she is.

—Anne Sullivan to Sophia Hopkins, April 1887

Night finds me in the rocker once again, humming to the Perkins doll as I mull over the day. I've given up weaning myself from the doll. By day she's Helen's plaything, victim to her indifference. At night she's my darling. I can't resist her when I settle into the rocking chair. Part of me curls with embarrassment at such childishness, but I pay no mind. It's a harmless pleasure, and I have so few. Since Mildred, and now Leila's little girl, have dipped into the wells of my affection, I can't bear sealing myself off again.

These days rolling one after the other with nothing happening are unbearable. I can feel myself shifting inside my skin, aching to move. Forward, backward, anything but this festering restlessness. It's been nearly a month since I arrived in Alabama, and what have I managed to accomplish?

And yet watching Leila's daughter today gave me some small hope. It's clear that language has found its way into her head, but her mouth isn't quite capable of giving it a way out. For a child like that it's only a matter of time until her muscles catch up with her brain. With Helen it's just the opposite. Her hand hasn't connected with her mind. She's like a baby babbling, intrigued by the shapes she can make, the way infants are fascinated by the first meaningless chirrups of their own voices. But she never makes the words unless I prompt her. I can only drop them into her hand like pebbles into a puddle, praying one day their meaning will spill across the rim of her mind.

This constant, thankless labor drains me. Receiving nothing in return weakens me like dry rot, yet keeping my warmth locked inside leaves me every bit as hollow. I don't know how much longer I can give of myself with no way to replenish what I've lost.

My head droops, weary with discouragement. I look down at the doll in my arms. Her flawless china face beams back at me. What would it be like to love a normal child, a child as perfect as this? In all my life I've never had a love that lasted. My mother, gone before I lost my milk teeth. My baby brothers and sisters, all stricken with one malady or another. Dear, dear Jimmie. And now Helen.

She's the same age Jimmie was when he died, Helen is. And just his size. Looking at her, I can't help remembering how tightly Jimmie and I held on to each other at Tewksbury. It was such a comfort, having someone familiar to cling to. "Oh, Jimmie," I whisper, trying to recall the soothing words I read so long ago at Perkins: "I would not wish any companion in the world but you; nor can I imagine a shape, besides your own, to love." I wonder if I'll ever know such closeness again.

Closing my eyes, I try to imagine away the doll's brittle hands and face, her slight cotton body. I dream of her as a child, my child—perfect in body and mind as Helen is not, and I never was. A child I could nourish, love, and teach with nothing but my own heart and hands.

A child who loves me back.

Next morning I turn up my nose at the table by the window and steer Helen into the garden for her lesson. She seems puzzled by the breach in routine. While I fasten her hat strings under her chin, I recite, by way of explanation:

> When thoughts
> . . . .
> And breathless darkness, and the narrow house,
> Make thee to shudder, and grow sick at heart;—
> Go forth under the open sky, and list
> To Nature's teachings.

As we work, the breezes wash us with the scent of honeysuckle and similax. Everything is growing and blooming and glowing. I suppose I hope Helen's mind will blossom outdoors too.

To encourage her interest, I scatter our familiar objects throughout a small section of the flower beds and hedges in front of the little house, letting her search for them. Like a foraging bear, Helen snuffles and roots through the brush, identifying her discoveries for me in exchange for a nibble of cake. Then I add a new set of objects: knife, fork, spoon, and saucer. When she dashes from place to place, I follow her, spelling *r-u-n* into her palm. Before the day is out, she's learned to spell eight new words.

The next day I turn the game about. Once she's located everything, I scatter the things back through the garden. I spell a word to Helen, then send her off in search of it, a mixture of hide-and-seek and fetch.

It doesn't work nearly as well; with nothing tangible in reach, Helen doesn't know what to do with the words. In the end I trail her from place to place, dropping the words into her hands just before she reaches an object.

From her flower beds Mrs. Keller watches us flit from one corner of the lawn to the other, a wistful smile on her face. I've noticed that expression before—when she watches me fastening Helen's napkin round her neck, straightening her pinafore, smoothing her hair. It's as if she's admiring something that flickers just out of reach. Seeing Mrs. Keller's half-bitten smile makes my chest squeeze. Her mouth looks so much more vulnerable than the rest of her, as if her every sorrow has settled there. Nothing as perceptible as a line stands out round her lips, only a sense of the effort it must take for her to sustain her cheer.

When Helen returns to my side, I spell *m-o-t-h-e-r*, and give her a gentle shove toward Mrs. Keller. With nothing more to guide her, Helen stumbles along at first, crashing through the ivy until her nose recognizes a familiar scent. Blind as a newborn kitten, she finds her way to Mrs. Keller by instinct, it seems. What could it be that pulls Helen toward her mother—the scent of roses, a lingering odor of the kitchen, a whiff of talcum powder? *Perhaps something deeper, more elemental,* I think. Could it be the same something that threaded Jimmie and me so tightly to one another? I watch Helen and Mrs. Keller embrace, my arms flattened to my sides. Will anyone ever feel that way for me again? My throat tightens as if it's filling with sand.

But the gesture buys me some goodwill from Mrs. Keller. After that she invites us to join her when she tends the flower beds. Helen takes to the new arrangement rapidly. She loves to dig and play in the dirt like any other child. With a small trowel and bucket she tunnels through the yard with the vigor of a mole. Working alongside Mrs. Keller suits me as well—I enjoy her company, and she's the most skillful gardener I've ever known. Already her sturdy rosebushes and vines are thick with nubby buds. When I was a child, we had only one smear of color in our drab blur of a house–a geranium that bloomed in the window. The nearest thing to gardening my mother ever did was strip the leaves from the poor thing. I pleaded with her not to do it, for I loved the feel of its furred leaves and the sharp smell they left on my hands, but she told me it was for my eyes. "Wash them," a neighbor had said, "in geranium water."

On my knees in the dirt with Mrs. Keller, the unspoken strain of my overtaking her place at Helen's side disappears for hours at a time. I watch our hands, working the soil in silent rhythm. My fingers look more stout and capable than I remember. A month of spelling for Helen has made them strong as dandelion roots. For the first time I prefer my rougher look to Mrs. Keller's grace.

As we gather our tools up before supper one evening, Helen tugs at my sleeve. With her trowel she points to the ground. Nestled between two azalea bushes the small hand of her rag doll reaches out from under a pile of turned earth.

"What in the world?" Mrs. Keller wonders.

Disgusted, I bend to retrieve the doll from her untimely grave, but Helen squats beside me, swatting my hands away. Protective, she lays her palm over the buried doll, then raises it, inch by inch, until she wobbles on tiptoe, reaching as high as my head.

"You cunning little thing," I laugh. "How did you ever put that together?"

Leaning on the handle of her spade, Mrs. Keller cocks her head. "What is it?"

"She's planted her doll. I think she expects it to grow as tall as I am." Together we laugh like schoolgirls as the sun ladles its warmth over our shoulders. Mrs. Keller pulls Helen to her side, smudging Helen's cheek with her dirt-stained touch. Trowel in hand, I follow them to the pump to wash up for supper.

"Wah-wah," Helen calls as the water gushes over her.

"Wah-wah, indeed," I sigh. "If only her mind could hear that word."

As they rinse their tools, I hang back, watching the sunlight glide over Helen's chestnut hair. It would feel hot and smooth as melted butter under my hands. Suddenly I understand the feeling that puts the wistful look on Mrs. Keller's face.

Later I try to bolster myself with Helen's lesson. Her success with "saucer," "knife," "fork," and "spoon" makes me wonder again why I can't get her to distinguish between "mug" and "milk." "Probably because I wasn't foolish enough to teach her 'food' and 'eat' at the same time," I chastise myself, laying out the cutlery. This time I add a cup to the arrangement. I also cut a handsome slice of cake and set it aside.

When Helen arrives for her lesson, I begin by putting the saucer in her hand. She beats out its name the instant I ask.

"Here's one I know you'll remember," I tell her, pressing Helen's hand into the spongy cake. After a few repetitions I place the slice of cake on the saucer and begin again.

"'Saucer.' Spell 'saucer.'" She spells it, and *c-a-k-e* when I ask for that. Back and forth between the two objects, she produces the words as I request. With "cake" and "saucer" there's no confusion.

Next I introduce the cup, drilling her over and over on the three nouns. She never falters. Finally I let her sniff the pitcher of milk I've brought upstairs, reminding her how to spell "milk." The pitcher bothers me—I wish there were a way to show her milk without a container—but it will have to do. Hopefully, the cup will be enough to untangle the mug-milk mess. Folding "milk" into the rotation, I continue drilling until I'm sure "milk" and "cup" are firmly embedded in her memory. To my immense satisfaction, she doesn't spell "mug" once.

As a test I pull the cup out of her reach and fill it with milk. Letting her touch only the outside of the object, I pat her fingers, asking for its name.

C-u-p.

I feed her a bite of cake, then hold the full cup under her nose. Almost thoughtfully she dips a finger in, then licks it.

M-i-l-k, her hand tells me when I ask.

I feel satisfaction widen my features. "'Milk,' conquered at last!"

Shoving the other articles aside, I grant Helen a fork and let her have her way with the entire slice of cake. It droops luxuriously over the rim of the saucer. I sit with my chin in my hand, watching her pile every crumb into her mouth. Once she's polished off the cake, and milk, too, I can't help rewarding myself with one last test.

With a flamboyant twist I scoop up the empty mug and place it before her. She inspects it briefly, and I present my hand for her pronouncement.

M-i-l-k.

My lips and brows shrink together, as if pulled by a drawstring. "Tell me that means you're thirsty," I say, pouring milk from the pitcher to the mug. As I hoped, she downs the milk in a single breath. Wary, but desperate to know, I direct her attention to the empty mug, patting her hand for the thousandth time.

M-i-l-k.

My confidence quailed, I put the cup in her hands. She feels the object before her carefully, then decides on "cup." I feel a thrill of relief, but I'm not so easily convinced. Dreading the answer, I give her the mug, to be certain. Her hands rove over its surface until I lay my hand over hers. I wince as she pauses after *m*. Her fingers falter under mine, shifting toward *i*, then back to *u*. I give them a steadying squeeze. Helen blinks twice, then finishes, resolute, with *i-l-k*.

I want to bury my head in my pillow and scream.

Chapter 28

*In a previous letter I think I wrote you that "mug" and
"milk" had given Helen more trouble than all the rest.*

—ANNE SULLIVAN TO SOPHIA HOPKINS, APRIL 1887

Long into the night I sit up, rocking. I feel as if my grip
on the Perkins doll is the only thing anchoring me to
this place. On the table the mug and cup stand out-
lined in the moonlight. The souring smell of leftover
milk hangs in the air.

I'm so frustrated I don't know what to do. It isn't
just the mug-milk mess. I've been here a month and
a day, and the fact is I still don't know how to be a
teacher to Helen. How do I show her what words are
without using words? And like a fool, I've nearly flung
Dr. Howe's system to the wind, though in all the world
there is no one else who can tell me how to break
through to this child.

I form my right fist into an *a* shape, cradling it
in my free hand. *A*, the humblest letter, the smallest

word. The simple shape of it, the meaning it carries, is a wonder to me. It fits so neatly into the hand of another. Silently I slip from my chair and creep to Helen's side of the bed. She sleeps spread out on her belly, one open palm tossed beside her pillow. My breathing shallow, I lower my fisted hand into hers. With my other hand I close her fingers over it, layering her small palm between mine.

For a moment I sit silently, my mind empty. With a deep breath I close my eyes and whisper, "*A.*"

The thought is firm in my mind. I imagine its electric pulse in my brain dissolving into my blood, traveling through the muscles of our clasped hands into Helen's mind. Squatting on my heels, I wait, as if for a fairy-tale ending: Helen's eyes fluttering open, lit from within, her feelings suddenly transformed into words.

But for the sound of my breathing, the room is silent.

Pressing our hands to my forehead, I whisper the name of the letter once again, willing the thought to pass through our skins.

Nothing.

Defeated and feeling foolish, I drop her hand and slink back to my chair. Minutes pass as I rock, trying to ignore the doll at my feet. She stares plaintively up at me; my misery is no secret from her. Finally I pull her up by one small hand. My arms close round her, nestling her golden hair against the hollow of my neck. Clutching the doll as if it were my own restless self, I finally drift off to sleep.

"Wah-wah," Helen bleats as the morning's wash water touches her hands. Bleary eyed, I wince at the harsh sound and continue scrubbing. She pats my hand.

"You're pleasing as a cloud of blackflies today," I tell her, but I spell *w-a-t-e-r* quickly as I can before yanking my hand away.

After breakfast I'm too tired to make our rounds through the outbuildings. Instead I pull Helen upstairs and flop into a chair, leaving her to her own devices.

At first she seems perplexed by the change in routine. Feeling round the room, she finds her hat and brings it to me.

I shake my head. "No," I tell her, tossing the hat aside. "We're not going outside."

Her hands drum across my body and the table, searching. A burst of exasperation cracks through my lips.

"Leave off, would you?" I bark, pushing her away. Her feet fumble backward over the Perkins doll. Distracted, she takes it up and commences her mechanized mothering.

She could sit and bore holes in the floor, for all I care. My eyes are so gritty and heavy lidded I don't want to do anything more than close them tight enough to shut out the world. Besides, each time I open them, I find nothing but that horrid mug staring back at me.

As Helen keens back and forth with the doll like an erratic pendulum, a droning hum buzzes in her throat. The noise creeps under my skin, rubbing like sandpaper. It swarms round me until I'm ready to shout.

At the crest of the rocker's movement I vault myself out of the chair and onto the floor. "There must be something I can teach you," I insist, kneeling before her like a dog on its haunches. On a stubborn impulse I reach up to the table and grab the mug. Pressing the cool ceramic against Helen's hand makes her face wrinkle up as she squirms away.

"My thoughts exactly." I set the mug aside and consider her. She rocks her china baby with fevered intensity. "So it's dolls today, is it?" I glance round the room to her heap of playthings. "Very well. We'll study dolls."

I crawl to the pile and pull at the first appendage I see. A large rag doll emerges from the mound of arms and legs. Returning to Helen, I plop down knee to knee in front of her and mirror her severe movements.

The combination of touch and motion attracts her attention. Still brandishing her doll in the crook of one elbow, Helen reaches across our laps to inspect me. When she's felt the rag doll, I slip a hand under hers and spell *d-o-l-l*.

She juts out her lip and jiggles her head as if a mosquito has landed there. Her hands return to the Perkins doll, and I watch them seek out all the subtle differences between the two toys. She lingers over the doll's thick coil of curls, her hard hands and face, the slick black boots painted on her pointed china toes.

Wedging my hand under hers, I spell again, *d-o-l-l*. This time she assents, imitating the letters.

"Good," I tell her, nodding. "But you're only halfway there. It means both one doll and every doll. It means 'doll' even if there isn't one in reach." Forgetting myself, I brush the back of my hand over her cheek. "That's the magic of it," I whisper.

With a sigh I pull my hand back and straighten myself. Businesslike once more, I switch the dolls from lap to lap, giving Helen the rag doll. Confusion makes her blink. With frenzied hands she slaps her palms over the doll's length. Realizing what I've done, she lets out a squawk and fumbles for my lap.

Reminded of my first encounter with Helen and her dolls, I shake my head. "Oh, no you don't. We're not starting that again." My emphatic movement subdues her, but her chest heaves under the weight of her vexation. I let her cool a moment, then point to the rag doll and pat her hand. Her fingers twitch once, but no letters come.

"It's easier than you think," I tell her, spelling "doll." Unconvinced, she nevertheless grunts and repeats my motions, then claims the china doll from my lap.

From this I create a game of give-and-take. We take turns as speller and doll keeper, bartering with words for possession of the playthings. Much to Helen's annoyance, no matter how resolute she makes the word, I persist in relinquishing the rag doll. No sooner does she get her hands on the coveted china doll than I take my turn to spell, compelling her to give up the only object she associates with the word–the Perkins doll.

After a quarter of an hour Helen huffs through gritted teeth. Her selfish nature roars within her, blotching her cheeks with red. Her bafflement inflames me as well. Heat rises in my veins each time Helen gives me the Perkins doll instead of its cloth cousin. The sound of each breath struggling past the lump in her throat fills me with sour pity.

"Keep it," I cry, shoving the china doll back into her arms. I spell "doll" again and jab at the rag doll draped across her knees. She shakes her head, as if it's brimming with undecipherable racket, and pushes the dolls away. Frustration gurgles out of her.

"Doll," I urge, bending her hands to feel both of them at once. She strains against me, but I force her hands nearer and nearer, the words slithering between my teeth. "Let me teach you. Let me–"

Her fists clutch at a handful of cloth on each doll's dress. With a scream like a diving gull Helen tears the dolls from me. The force of her anger jolts her backward like the kick of a rifle. For an instant the dolls hang in midair, their blank eyes serene. My breath stops. In one swift *whoosh* Helen slams her arms to the floor.

The Perkins doll shatters.

Chapter 29

*I must write you a line this morning because
something very important has happened.*

—Anne Sullivan to Sophia Hopkins, April 5, 1887

Shock leaves me paralyzed, hunched forward on my knees. My thoughts seem muffled by flannel rags. Somewhere within me outrage and grief roil, but I can't feel them. It's as if I'm floating above the waves, sheltered in a small boat on a dark sea. I only stare, fascinated, unable to understand why no blood runs from the doll's innumerable wounds.

Empty, I marvel to myself. *Empty as my own heart, and Helen's.*

Helen sits panting among the pieces, her rage spent. As her fingers walk through the fragments of the doll's smile, calm spreads over her face. Her remorseless inspection makes me queasy. Unperturbed, she reaches for the doll's severed neck. Jagged peaks of china jut beneath its lacy collar.

"No," I say, pulling Helen to her feet. "No blood."

Frantic, I take up the broom and sweep the bits of doll corpse to one side of the hearth, flinching at every clink and scrape.

Hands deadly calm, I prop the broom over the mess, trying to hide the broken bits. I don't know what to do. The room seems too small, too close. I don't trust my anger to stay hidden. Instinctively I reach out and brush a flake of porcelain from Helen's cheek. She raises her hand to feel the place I've touched. Shards of china glint like drops of milk on her bare arms.

"Don't move," I tell her, squeezing her shoulder. Scooping up the mug from the floor, I dash to the washbasin and fill it with water. I take Helen by the wrists and extend her arms, then pour the water down the length of them.

A startled cry of "wah-wah" erupts from her mouth, penetrating the cloudiness round my stifled mind. I look at the mug in my hand, the water dripping from Helen's splayed fingertips.

My thoughts leap forward, desperate to leave the image of the broken doll behind. "Water." She asked for the word herself this morning. Why didn't I think to use it before, with all my worries over cups and mugs and milk? Eager to grasp the distraction, I towel Helen dry with my own skirt, then yank her hat from the table and drop it on her head. With a start she feels the hat and grunts with satisfaction.

Outside the warm sunshine makes her skip and hop like a little frog. Her nose trembles in the soft air, drawing her to the honeysuckle that covers the pump house. Reaching it, she stretches to weave her fingers into the tangle of cool leaves.

I pull her aside and force the mug into her hand. She hisses between her teeth as if struck with a pain. "Like this," I demand, positioning the mug under the spout. I take a step back. Helen slouches. With a jerk I twist the mug about and reposition her. Another step back. She holds her pose. Joining our free hands, I catch hold of the pump handle, wincing at the heat of the sun-scorched paint.

I spell *w-a-t-e-r*, first slowly, then faster and faster as I work the handle. Suddenly a wide tongue of water gushes from the mouth of the pump.

"Wah—"

The sound twists into a gasp. She freezes. The mug drops, shattering on the packed dirt. Her hand clutches at mine. She stands transfixed, her whole attention focused on the motion of my fingers.

I feel a change in the way she grips my hand. Her muscles, so often limp with indifference, strain to catch each movement. My chest heaves as I realize the difference: She's listening, with every bone and fiber.

Something is happening inside her head.

The letters don't thud blankly into her palm. I feel them crackle through her skin, forging a lightning-path up the muscles in her arm. Her chin trembles. Light rinses over her face, smothering my momentary impulse to pat her hand.

Beneath the spout the fingers of her free hand move of their own accord.

Rigid with astonishment, Helen pulls my whole arm under the cold stream, spelling "water" again and again and yet again, begging me to understand.

My eyes well. "Water," I murmur, wrapping both my hands round hers.

W-a-t-e-r. I cradle the word like an egg in my hands, midwife to this single expression like nothing Helen has given voice to before—neither anger, satisfaction, nor desire. The weight of it chokes me.

I nod. "Yes." She spells the word once more to herself and nods. Amazement makes her motion slow, almost graceful, and I know she's realizing, as she never has before, how simple it can be to make the world understand anything in her mind. I feel a bursting: the flash of two minds meeting there in my palm.

In a frenzy Helen breaks free and drops to the ground. I stand for a moment, looking dumbly into my empty hands as if I expect to find something left behind—a broken shell, a withered cocoon? Pulsing with excitement, Helen slaps the wet earth at my feet, seizing my skirts like a desperate pauper.

I fall to my knees. She takes my hand, beats the muddy ground with it, then grabs at me to spell. My fingers won't make the letters fast enough. "G-r-o-u-n-d." In the space of a breath she spells the word to me, to herself, to the very ground beneath us.

Ravenous for more, Helen pulls me to the pump,

the trellis, anything within reach, tearing their names from my fingers. Her breath comes in great, choking gulps, like a crippled laugh. She throws her arms out wide, ready to embrace the world. Flinging herself round, her hands fall on me.

She stops still. Her fingers walk up to my face. I watch her throat bob with a heavy swallow. For the first time she seems unsure of herself. Softer now, she pats my cheek, then my hand.

Me. She wants to know what I am, in a single word.

I bite my lips as I spell out the letters: *t-e-a-c-h-e-r*.

"Teacher," I say, pulling her small hand to my breast. "Teacher." She nods.

Just then the nursemaid comes into the pump house carrying Mildred. Touching her sister, Helen gropes for my hand, then halts. Her head snaps toward the sky, struck by another realization.

B-a-b-y, she spells, and touches my face. Wild with pride, I jerk my head up and down. "Yes."

Helen's face shines as though she's cracked open a cask of jewels. I imagine the dozens of words she's copied in oblivious imitation for all these weeks suddenly bursting to life inside her mind. Reeling with possibilities, she tumbles toward the house, hands flailing for objects to name.

A laugh burbles up inside me, and I shout after her, "Helen!"

My hands rise to my mouth. Five weeks, and this is the first time I've called Helen by her name.

Staggering up from my knees, I rush to her side. I take hold of her wrists, commanding her to be still. With wavering hands I place her palm over her breast-bone and hold it in place as I spell.

H-e-l-e-n.

Through the stillness I feel her heart fluttering against her ribs. Moving her fingers carefully as if they might break, she repeats the letters of her name, then pats her chest, once.

"Yes," I whisper, nodding. "Yes—Helen."

Her eyes glow like opals with the tears.

Chapter 30

I didn't finish my letter in time to get it posted
last night; so I shall add a line.

—Anne Sullivan to Sophia Hopkins, April 5, 1887

All through the yard and house we race, Helen gobbling the fledgling words like nectar. Her unending appetite, her clinging eagerness, thrills me, making every touch seem a caress. Everything our hands fall upon feels new and alive; her face grows brighter with each new name.

Until she finds the fragments of the Perkins doll.

In our room she makes her way to the hearth, where the doll clatters under her boots. Bending down, she touches the fragments. Her mouth pleats as she tries to piece the doll back together. When the bits won't join, she plops to the floor, and her little face falls. Tears the size of raindrops roll from her eyes.

The sight of Helen crying for that doll twists my heart and makes it dance, till I cry too, though not for the doll. No word I could spell to her would ease the pain. I can only sit down beside her and brush the tears from her cheeks, begging her, "Don't cry, love, don't cry. She doesn't matter anymore."

By nightfall my body thrums with exhilaration. If I'd ever seen a child born, it couldn't compare to what happened at the pump today. Helen opened before my eyes, and whatever it is that makes us human flowed into her as if I'd poured it from my own hands.

As I help her undress for bed, I spell the name of each of her garments. "Pinafore," "dress," "shoes," "stockings," "nightdress." Climbing into the bed itself, she learns "sheet," "quilt," "mattress," "spread," and "pillow." I cover her up and cleave our hands apart. Helen stretches toward me, troubled by the separation. Our fingers have been tangled together since we left the pump, it seems.

Her distress touches a long-neglected place in the center of me. I know Helen needs me, perhaps more than I ever needed her. Our connection runs deeper than affection, for without my hand in hers, she sinks into darkness and silence, the depth of which she's only today begun to fathom. I give her hand a squeeze, tucking a rag doll under the sheet for company.

"I'll be right there, dear," I whisper, brushing the hair from her flushed cheek. The severity of her sudden dependence astounds me; her thirst for the world burns in her skin, and only I can quench it for her.

And yet I want to give her more than myself. I want to see the word-seeds I drop into her hands blossom into ideas. I want to learn the patterns of her mind. To watch Helen discover her thoughts—her self—once more.

Quickly I undress and slip under the covers. Helen's hand finds mine in the dark. I wait for her to spell, to ask for one more word. Instead she scumbles her fingers across my face, pausing for a moment at the teardrop-shaped hollow above my lips. Wriggling nearer, she steals into my arms and presses her lips to my cheek.

I think my heart will burst with the joy that floods it.

I close my arms round her, feel her warm weight against me, and I know—this child is mine, and I am hers. She is not of my body, but I am mother to Helen's heart and mind.

H-e-l-e-n, I spell into her listening palm. The feel of it is like a prayer between my fingers.

T-e-a-c-h-e-r, she answers.

Teacher. She's only begun to grasp the breadth of it, and already that one word stirs my very bones. My heart falls open before her, ready to be fashioned by her two small hands.

H-e-l-e-n a-n-d T-e-a-c-h-e-r, I spell back. I hardly know how to begin telling her what or how much this means.

But I shall try. However long it takes, I shall try.

AFTERWORD

About Annie and Helen

Anne Sullivan was twenty years old on the day she met Helen Keller–a day Helen would celebrate ever after as her "soul's birthday." Within a month Annie had broken through to Helen by making her understand the miracle of language. From that moment at the water pump until Annie's death in 1936, Helen called Annie by no other name but "Teacher."

For the next fifty years Annie rarely left Helen's side. Her pupil would become an international celebrity, lecturer, writer, and activist, while Annie was often overlooked and literally pushed aside. In spite of it all, her loyalty never faltered. Anchored by Helen's unwavering devotion, Annie remained capricious, contrary, lively, and courageous almost to the end.

In 1904 Helen became the first deaf-blind person to earn a college degree, but it was Annie who had spelled four years of classroom lectures and textbooks into Helen's hands. While she was still in college, *Ladies' Home Journal* commissioned Helen to write her autobiography. The book became a classic, and its editor, John Macy, became Annie's husband. For almost nine years the three lived together as a family. From 1913 until 1923 Helen and Annie toured the United States and Canada, giving speeches and lectures, and performing on the vaudeville circuit. In 1918 they even made a silent film, called *Deliverance*.

Beginning in 1916 Annie's health began to falter. Her eyesight dimmed, and she developed what doctors feared was tuberculosis—the same disease that had killed Jimmie at Tewksbury. For the first and only time in their lives Helen and Annie were separated for five months when Annie was sent to Puerto Rico, in hopes of recovering her strength. It was only a temporary fix.

During the 1920s, as Helen campaigned tirelessly for the blind, Polly Thomson, hired in 1914 as the pair's secretary, slowly began to take over Annie's position as Helen's public companion. By 1933 Annie was virtually blind and growing frail, though she told Helen, "I am trying so hard to live for you."

The last words Annie spoke, recorded by Polly Thomson on October 15, 1936, were of her brother Jimmie, and then Helen: "God help her to live without me when I go." Soon after, Annie slipped into a coma; she died five days later, with Helen holding her hand.

Upon her death in 1936 Anne Sullivan became the first woman to be interred in the National Cathedral in Washington, DC, on her own merits. Monuments to her memory stand around the world—even the somewhat dubious honor of a building and sculpture in her name at Tewksbury. In 1932 Helen had persuaded her to accept an honorary degree from Temple University.

Though the loss of her beloved teacher shook Helen to her core, she would live another thirty years, writing books (including her own biography of Annie, called simply *Teacher*), giving speeches, and raising funds for the blind until she was eighty years old, outliving even Polly Thomson. Helen Keller died in 1968, just short of her eighty-eighth birthday.

To the world Helen Keller will always be something of a miracle. But to Helen, Annie Sullivan, "Teacher," was the world. As Helen herself wrote:

Teacher, and yet again
Teacher—and that was all.
It will be my answer
In the dark
When Death calls.

About This Book

During her first year in Tuscumbia, Annie wrote regularly to her housemother at Perkins. Though a leaking roof reduced the originals to pulp, extensive excerpts of Annie's letters survive in the original and restored editions of Helen's autobiography *The Story of My Life*. The bulk of this novel is based on those letters, and they are the source of the quotes at the head of each chapter. For the stories of Annie and Jimmie's life in Tewksbury, I referred almost exclusively to *Anne Sullivan Macy*, a biography written by Nella Braddy Henney just three years before Annie's death. A close friend to both Annie and Helen, Nella was the first person to whom Annie confided the stories of her years at the almshouse; even Helen herself knew nothing of the shame of Tewksbury until 1926.

It's rather a presumptuous thing to write someone else's story—even more so to try to write it in her own voice. The best any author of this sort of book can hope to do is present the truth as he or she sees it. I am grateful that Annie herself knew this and said so to Nella Braddy Henney: "The truth of a matter is not what I tell you about it, but what you divine in regard to it." I have kept this thought in my mind during the whole writing of this book. What you have read is what I have divined and what I believe to be emotionally true. In her own way, I believe Annie would approve.

Although I was as faithful as possible to the historical record, there is one intentional wrinkle in the time line I must confess to: "Bessie's Song to Her Doll," the rhyme about a doll called Matilda Jane, was not written by Lewis Carroll until 1893—a full six years after this novel is set. However, the poem was so appropriate to the story I just couldn't resist including it.

—S. M.

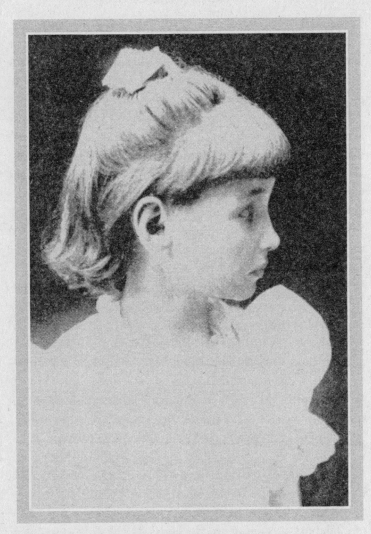

The earliest surviving photo of Helen Keller, taken at age seven. No pictures of Helen before the arrival of Annie Sullivan are known to exist. *Courtesy of the American Foundation for the Blind, Helen Keller Archives*

The earliest known photo of Anne Sullivan, taken in 1881, within a year of her arrival at the Perkins Institution. She was fifteen years old. *Courtesy of the Perkins School for the Blind*

Anne Sullivan, photographed on August 1, 1887, a few months after her breakthrough with Helen. *Courtesy of the Perkins School for the Blind*

Annie and Helen fingerspelling together in 1890. This is one of a handful of photos showing Helen's protruding left eye. For many years, she was carefully photographed in profile to hide the deformity. *Courtesy of the Perkins School for the Blind*

The main gate to the old Tewksbury State Almshouse grounds as it looks today. The administration building has become the Massachusetts Public Health Museum.

Reg. No. 48457 - 458   Age 10
Name Annie Sullivan

48458 James   5, born Agawam
    Hip Disease

From Agawam Feb. 22, 1876
Condition Weak Eyes
Examined March 29, 1876
[48458 (James) Died May 30, 1876]

Discharged
Removed
By whom
For Nos.

10, born July 1866, Agawam, and always lived there till sent here. Father Thomas Sullivan, born Ireland. No estate, can't tell if naturalized or paid taxes, or in service in [Civil] War. Now lives in Agawam, working as a farmer for Stephen O'Hearn. Mother Alice died about 2 years ago in Agawam. Sister Mary, 3 years old, with Aunt Mary Clacey in Agawam. Sore eyes, and James has hip complaint. Neither ever went to school.

The page of the almshouse ledger recording Jimmie and Annie's arrival at Tewksbury and outlining a few facts about their family life. A notation of Jimmie's death on May 30, 1876, was later squeezed in between lines.

Workers in the almshouse laundry. *Courtesy of the Tewksbury Historical Society*

The Perkins Institution for the Blind, as it appeared in 1904.
Courtesy of the Perkins School for the Blind

A classroom at Perkins, circa 1890. The U-shaped arrangement of desks was typical of Perkins. *Courtesy of the Perkins School for the Blind*

Ivy Green, and the little house, as they appear today. *Photo by Larry Gillentine © 1995*

The water pump at Ivy Green, silhouetted against the kitchen building. *Photo by Sarah Miller © 2007*

More Information

Books

The Story of My Life by Helen Keller (restored editions
   including Annie's letters have been published by Modern
   Library and W. W. Norton)
Anne Sullivan Macy by Nella Braddy Henney
Teacher by Helen Keller
Helen and Teacher by Joseph P. Lash
The World I Live In by Helen Keller
Helen Keller: Rebellious Spirit by Laurie Lawlor

Online

Perkins online museum, Anne Sullivan history section:
   www.perkins.org/museum/section.php?id=214
American Foundation for the Blind's Anne Sullivan Macy
   museum: www.afb.org/annesullivan/
Tewksbury Historical Society archives, Tewksbury
   Almshouse section:
   http://www.tewksburyhistoricalsociety.org/Archives/
   StateHospital/index.html (includes an excerpt from
   Anne Sullivan Macy)
AFB's Helen Keller museum: www.afb.org/Section.
   asp?SectionID=1

AFB's Braille Bug, an interactive kids' museum of
    Helen Keller: www.afb.org/braillebug/hkmuseum.asp
    (a clip of the only existing recording of Annie's voice
    can be found at www.afb.org/braillebug/
    hkgallery.asp?tpid=3)
Ivy Green's official website:
    www.helenkellerbirthplace.org

VIDEOS

Helen Keller in Her Story (originally released in the
    1950s as *The Unconquered*)
The Miracle Worker (I particularly recommend the 1962
    version, starring Anne Bancroft and Patty Duke)

Chronology

April 14, 1866—Johanna "Annie" Sullivan is born in Feeding Hills, Massachusetts.

1874—Annie's mother dies.

February 22, 1876—Annie and Jimmie enter Tewksbury.

May 30, 1876—Jimmie dies.

June 27, 1880—Helen Keller is born in Tuscumbia, Alabama.

October 7, 1880—Annie enters Perkins Institution for the Blind.

February 1882—Helen becomes deaf and blind.

August 1886—The Kellers write to Perkins, requesting a teacher.

March 3, 1887—Annie arrives in Tuscumbia and meets Helen.

April 5, 1887—Helen learns "water."

1900—Helen enters Radcliffe College.

1902—Annie and Helen meet John Macy.

1903—Helen publishes *The Story of My Life*.

1904—Helen graduates cum laude from Radcliffe College.

May 2, 1905—Annie marries John Macy.

1913-16—Annie and Helen tour the North American lecture circuit.

1914—Annie and John Macy separate; Polly Thomson is hired.

1916—Helen nearly elopes; Annie's health begins to fail, and she spends five months in Puerto Rico.

1918—Annie and Helen travel to Hollywood to film *Deliverance*.

1919-23—Annie and Helen perform on the vaudeville circuit.

1929—Annie's right eye is removed.

1932—John Macy dies; Annie's health sinks further, and she becomes virtually blind.

February 16, 1932—Annie and Helen receive honorary degrees from Temple University.

1933—*Anne Sullivan Macy* is published.

October 20, 1936—Annie dies.

1955—Helen publishes *Teacher*.

1960—Polly Thomson dies.

June 1, 1968—Helen dies.

Sources Consulted

BOOKS AND ARTICLES

Braddy, Nella. *Anne Sullivan Macy: The Story Behind Helen Keller*. Garden City, NY: Doubleday, Doran, 1933.

Gibson, William. *The Miracle Worker*. New York: Bantam, 1960.

Gritter, Elizabeth. *The Imprisoned Guest: Samuel Howe and Laura Bridgman*. New York: Farrar, Strauss and Giroux, 2001.

Harrity, Richard, and Ralph G. Martin. *The Three Lives of Helen Keller*. Garden City, NY: Doubleday, 1962.

Herrmann, Dorothy. *Helen Keller: A Life*. New York: Knopf, 1998.

Howe, Maud, and Florence Howe Hall. *Laura Bridgman: Dr. Howe's Famous Pupil and What He Taught Her*. Boston: Little, Brown, 1904.

Keirsey, David, and Marilyn Bates. *Please Understand Me: Character and Temperament Types*. Del Mar, CA: Prometheus Nemesis, 1984.

Keller, Helen. *Helen Keller's Journal*. New York: Doubleday, 1938.

———. *Midstream: My Later Life*. New York: Doubleday, 1929.

———. *The Story of My Life*. Edited by James Berger. New York: Modern Library, 2003.

———. *The Story of My Life: The Restored Classic*. Edited by Roger Shattuck, with Dorothy Herrmann. New York: W. W. Norton, 2003.

———. *Teacher*. New York: Doubleday, 1955.

———. *The World I Live In*. New York: Century, 1908.

Konigsburg, E. L. *Talktalk: A Children's Book Author Speaks to Grown-ups*. New York: Atheneum, 1995.

Lamson, Mary Swift. *Life and Education of Laura Dewey Bridgman*. Boston: New England Publishing, 1879.

Lash, Joseph P. *Helen and Teacher: The Story of Helen Keller and Anne Sullivan Macy*. New York: Delacorte, 1980.

Paterson, Katherine. *Gates of Excellence: On Reading and Writing Books for Children*. New York: Elsevier/Nelson Books, 1981.

Percy, Walker. *The Message in the Bottle: How Queer Man Is, How Queer Language Is, and What One Has to Do with the Other*. New York: Farrar, Strauss and Giroux, 1975.

Tilney, Frederick. "A Comparative Sensory Analysis of Helen Keller and Laura Bridgman." *Archives of Neurology and Psychiatry*, June 1929, 1227–69.

FILMS

Helen Keller: In Her Story. VHS. Directed and produced by Nancy Hamilton. N.p.:Hen's Tooth Video, 1992.

The Miracle Worker. DVD. N.p.: Playfilm Productions, 1962.

ONLINE SOURCES

Brown, Jonathan, et al. "Eighth Annual Report of the Inspectors of the State Almshouse at Tewksbury." Boston, MA: William White, 1861. http://www.tewksburyhistoricalsociety.org/Archives/StateHospital/index.html (accessed March 24, 2006).

Butler, Benjamin. "Argument Before the Tewksbury Investigation Committee." Boston, MA: Democratic Central Committee, 1883. http://www.tewksburyhistoricalsociety.org/Archives/StateHospital/index.html (accessed March 24, 2006).

"Cartoons and Comments." *Puck Magazine*, August 1, 1883: 342. http://www.tewksburyhistoricalsociety.org/Archives/StateHospital/index.html (accessed March 24, 2006).

Davis, R. T., et al. "Fifth Annual Report of the State Board of Health, Lunacy, and Charity of the State of Massachusetts." Boston, MA: Wright & Potter Printing Co., 1884. http://www.tewksburyhistoricalsociety.org/Archives/StateHospital/index.html (accessed March 25, 2006).

Leonard, Clara T. "The Present Condition of Tewksbury." Boston, MA: Franklin Press, 1883. http://www.tewksburyhistoricalsociety.org/Archives/StateHospital/index.html (accessed March 24, 2006).

"The Record of Benjamin F. Butler Since His Election as Governor of Massachusetts." Boston, MA: 1883. http://www.tewksburyhistoricalsociety.org/Archives/StateHospital/index.html (accessed March 25, 2006).

Acknowledgments

I owe a debt of thanks to a great many people:

All those who encouraged this story, and the ones that came before it: Aunt Alice, Miriam Burkhart, Judy & Rich Dugger, Richard Hill, Sharon Lark, Judy Lopus, William Menter, Aleda Morr, Mary Payne, Linda Pavonetti, Christine Rowley, Cynthia Sanborn, and the staff of the "old" Kezar Library.

My early readers: Carol Azizian, Ruth Burns, Collyn & Daryl DeBano, Cherrill Flynn, and Sue Sirgany.

For their support and general bookishness, my fine friends at Halfway Down the Stairs: Linda Brick, Sue Lorenzen, Cam Mannino, Martha Nelson, and Pat Penney.

Casey Leigh Floyd, who writes the best post-rejection consolation e-mails ever!

Kelly DiPucchio and Sue Stauffacher, for leading me to my agent.

Erica Stahler, who saved me from a handful of embarrassing errors, and Kim Nielsen for giving me a passing grade on my "Annie Sullivan Final" with her insightful reading of the manuscript.

Wendy Schmalz and Justin Chanda, my agent and my editor, who never made me feel like a rookie.

Donna Jo Napoli, who has been a Teacher to me.

And Mom & Dad, who took me to Meadow Brook Theatre to see *The Miracle Worker*, and then said, "Let's go to Alabama."

Enter the world of Russia's last royal sisters . . .

Lost Crown

By Sarah Miller

Available in June 2011

MARIA NIKOLAEVNA

June 1914

There has never been such a summer! Since sailing from Peterhof, my sisters and I have spent all day on the sunny decks of our dear *Standart*, playing shuffleboard, rollerskating, dancing, and yes, sometimes flirting with the officers. Of course, they kissed our hands when we climbed aboard, but only because we're the tsar's daughters—they can't simply wave hello to a flock of grand duchesses. None of the four of us has had a real kiss, unless one of my sisters has suddenly started keeping secrets.

The only dark blot on our trip is Aleksei's accident. Three days ago, our brother knocked his ankle on a rung of the ship's ladder. Instead of scampering about the decks with his spaniel in his starched sailor suit, the poor darling ended up stranded in bed, the joint twisted and swelling by the minute. Mama's sent three telegrams to *Otyets* Grigori, hoping the holy man's prayers will cure our little Sunbeam. In the meantime, Anastasia, Tatiana, and I tease our oldest sister, Olga, mercilessly about her matches with Crown Prince Carol of Romania and our cousin David, the prince of Wales. Even the ship's officers join in.

Clearing her throat, Tatiana straightens up, her hands clasped behind her back. "I am requested by the officers of His Majesty's yacht *Standart* to present this card to Her Imperial Highness, the Grand Duchess Olga Nikolaevna," she announces, handing over an envelope with a little curtsy.

I peek at Anastasia. Something's up; we never use our

titles amongst each other, and neither do the officers. Anastasia only shrugs, but you can never tell with her. Our impish little sister could very well be behind this.

Olga pulls a card out of the envelope. "Oh!" she says after hardly a glimpse, her hands flying to her hips. "It was you, wasn't it, *Shvybzik*?" she demands, shaking the card at Anastasia.

"Not me," Anastasia insists, batting her eyelashes before she ducks under Olga's hand and snatches the card away. She glances at it and snorts with laughter. Behind us the officers chuckle as Anastasia capers about the deck, waving the card like a banner. Tatiana's dogs, Jemmy and Ortipo, yip and prance along.

"You all are swine!" Olga declares. I've no choice but to catch Anastasia and read over her shoulder.

The joke's a good one: a cutout newspaper photo of cousin David's head pasted onto a picture of Michelangelo's *David*–that huge naked statue! I can't help hooting right along with Anastasia.

"Oh, Nastya, what a pair they'll make! Him stark naked and Olga in the fifteen-pound silver nightgown of a grand duchess, just like Auntie Ksenia had to wear on her wedding night!"

"Humpf." Olga sniffs at me. "You're just as much a grand duchess as I am, Mashka, and you'll be fitted for your own fifteen-pound nightgown one of these days. If we can only find someone willing to marry our fat little Bow-Wow!"

"Of course I'll marry," I sing out. "I'll marry a soldier and have dozens of children."

"And they'll be prettier than yours, Olga," Anastasia pipes up, "because her babies will all have Mashka's big blue saucer-eyes." I clasp Anastasia around the waist and peck her cheek. She's a *shvybzik*, but she knows my dreams as well as I do.

"Fine, we can set a banquet table with Mashka's saucers."

Tatiana bursts out laughing, and the officers applaud Olga.

At the sound of a sob from Aleksei's rooms below decks, the smile leaves Tatiana's face. Our giggles dissolve in a heartbeat. We all look at each other, thinking the same thing: that time it sounded like Mama. Suddenly somber, the officers shift their eyes to the deck. Tatiana hurries past them all, her skirts fluttering like sails behind her. Olga follows, and Anastasia and I fall into line, hand in hand and a trifle skittish. Stranded at the top of the stairs, Jemmy whines, her little legs too stubby to follow us down the steps.

We find Tatiana with Mama in the passageway outside Aleksei's cabin. Mama's face is pale and her cheeks streaked with tears. As we come closer, she leans her head on Tatiana's shoulder and closes her eyes. Beside me Anastasia stiffens. "What's wrong?" she asks.

Tatiana puts a finger to her lips and motions us toward Aleksei's doorway. "Go in," she whispers. Her eyes flick down to a rumpled telegram in Mama's hand. "No one has told him."

Olga nods and steps ahead. I take a breath and pull Anastasia along behind me. Nagorny, Aleksei's sailor-nanny, nods, then shuts the door silently behind us. Our brother's *dyadka* always makes me relax a little. Having Nagorny nearby is like sitting under a birch tree, he's so tall and steady in his white sailor suit.

Inside the cool, dim cabin, Joy, Aleksei's spaniel, thumps his tail at us but doesn't budge from his place beside our brother's bunk. Only Aleksei's eyes stand out from the bedclothes. His face and hands have begun to turn waxy-white. Under the sheet his ankle bulges, already swollen as big as his knee. The pull of the sheet as Olga sits on the edge of the bed makes him wince. A hollow opens in my chest at the sight of him like that.

"How are you, Sunbeam?" I ask, leaning over to kiss his dear little forehead and slip a candy from my pocket under his pillow.

"Better than yesterday," he says, his voice as small as his face, "but still swelling."

Still swelling! If I'd knocked my ankle on that ladder, I'd have no more to endure than an ugly bruise and my sisters' teasing about my clumsiness. Poor Aleksei has lain in bed three days, and the blood is still pooling into the joint.

"Where's Tatiana?" he asks.

Olga and I look uneasily at each other, but Anastasia springs into action.

"Oh, you know 'the Governess.' She's probably discussing your lessons with Monsieur Gilliard this very minute." Anastasia stands on her toes and stretches out her neck to make herself as tall as our regal Tatiana. "Monsieur Gilliard," she says, addressing me with a twinkle in her eyes, "Aleksei is neglecting his studies. Something must be done."

"But Tatiana Nikolaevna, " I begin, and as I try to bow, Anastasia takes one of Aleksei's sailor hats from the bed and pushes its long black ribbon against my upper lip to imitate our tutor's wide mustache. Aleksei blinks with amusement, and Anastasia presses on.

"Really, Monsieur, he has lolled about in bed three days now. It is positively disgraceful."

"But surely, Your Highness," I say, bowing again and gesturing to Aleksei's bed. But I forget to keep hold of my mustache, and the sailor hat topples to the floor. Olga shakes her head and rolls her eyes, but Anastasia keeps up the charade.

"My dear Monsieur," she huffs, "that will be quite enough. I see I have underestimated you. A man who cannot even keep track of his own mustache simply cannot be capable of educating the next tsar of the Russias. You are dismissed!"

I let my head fall to my chest and make my way to the door.

Anastasia yanks the hat from the carpet and holds it out to me, one ribbon pinched between two fingers and her pinky sticking out a *verst*. "And take this with you. I will not have discarded mustaches lying about the tsarevich's bedroom!"

Aleksei smiles, a real smile this time, and bursts into applause. Olga joins in after an instant while Anastasia and I hold hands and curtsy.

At that very moment, Monsieur Gilliard himself appears in the doorway, his arms full of our brother's favorite storybooks. Aleksei explodes with laughter, and the pinch of happiness inside my chest splits open like a firecracker. Anastasia turns white for a flash, then grabs me by the arm and pulls me straight under Monsieur's mustache and into the corridor, slamming the door on our tutor's bewildered face. Despite Mama's startled glance and Tatiana's glare, I can't help wrapping my arms around my clown of a little sister with a hug that lifts her from her feet. Even though I know something dreadful has happened, for that moment, the only thing I can think of is that I love Anastasia best of all.

Don't miss any of these amazing novels from the winner of the National Book Award and the Newbery Medal,

CYNTHIA KADOHATA:

PRINT AND EBOOK EDITIONS AVAILABLE   KIDS.SimonandSchuster.com

Check out these stories by National Book Award finalist
TOR SEIDLER,
who shows us that everyone's different, and that's wonderful!

Margaret is mean. She's loud! She's rude! But two woodchucks take in Margaret as their own, despite her horrible tendencies. Will Margaret ever be nice?

The dashing Wainscott Weasel isn't like the other weasels. Instead he is smitten by the most unlikely of creatures. . . .

Lamar is the son of the alpha male. But he is no ordinary wolf, for he sees the beauty in the world—and in a coyote. It seems that no matter what he decides to do, he will let someone down—his father, a coyote the entire pack, even himself . . .

PRINT AND EBOOK EDITIONS AVAILABL

atheneum   KIDS.SimonandSchuster.co

IRRESISTIBLE FICTION
— *from Edgar Award–winning author* —
FRANCES O'ROARK DOWELL!

ANYBODY SHINING

THE SECRET LANGUAGE OF GIRLS

THE KIND OF FRIENDS WE USED TO BE

THE SOUND OF YOUR VOICE . . . ONLY REALLY FAR AWAY

THE SECOND LIFE OF ABIGAIL WALKER

FALLING IN

DOVEY COE

WHERE I'D LIKE TO BE

CHICKEN BOY

SHOOTING THE MOON

Atheneum

SimonandSchuster.com/kids
PRINT *and* EBOOK EDITIONS AVAILABLE

what if no one could hear you?
would they think you had nothing to say?

Melody has a photographic memory. She remembers every word that is spoken around her and every fact she has ever learned. Melody also has cerebral palsy, and is entirely unable to communicate. It's enough to make a girl go out of her mind.

From award-winning author **Sharon M. Draper** comes a book as heartbreaking as it is hopeful, about a girl you'll never forget.

From Atheneum Books for Young Readers
Published by Simon & Schuster
KIDS.SimonandSchuster.com

PRINT AND EBOOK EDITIONS ALSO AVAILABLE

The story of one girl's unrelenting quest for freedom.

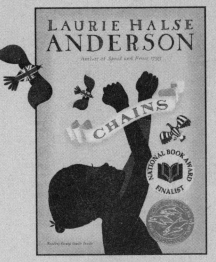

**NATIONAL BOOK
AWARD FINALIST**

**WINNER OF THE
SCOTT O'DELL AWARD
FOR HISTORICAL
FICTION**

* "Startlingly provocative . . . nuanced and evenhanded . . .
a fast-moving, emotionally involving plot."
—*Publishers Weekly*, starred review

* "Anderson explores elemental themes of power, freedom, and the
sources of human strength in this searing, fascinating story."
—*Booklist*, starred review

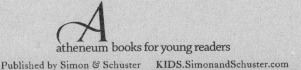

atheneum books for young readers

Published by Simon & Schuster   KIDS.SimonandSchuster.com